Kill Two Birds
& Get Stoned

Kill Two Birds
& Get Stoned

Kinky Friedman

LARGE PRINT

This large print edition published in 2003 by
RB Large Print
A division of Recorded Books
A Haights Cross Communications Company
270 Skipjack Road
Prince Frederick, MD 20678

Previously published by William Morrow,
an imprint of HarperCollinsPublishers, 2003

Publisher's Cataloging In Publication Data
(Prepared by Donohue Group, Inc.)

Friedman, Kinky.
  Kill two birds & get stoned / Kinky Friedman.

    p. ; cm.

  Other title. Kill two birds and get stoned
  ISBN: 1–4025–6382–5

1. Fiction—Authorship—Fiction. 2. Novelists—Fiction. 3. Large type
books. 4. Humorous fiction. 5. Satire. I. Title. II. Title: Kill two
birds and get stoned.

PS3556.R527 K55 2003b
813/ .54

Typeset by Palimpsest Book Production Limited
Polmont, Stirlingshire, Scotland
Printed in the United States of America
by Bang Printing
3323 Oak Street
Brainerd, Minnesota 56401

This book is dedicated to Steve Rambam, who inspired and guided it; to Dwight Yoakam, who believed in it; and to the memory of Iru Rubin, who lived it

It is a better thing by far that the lad should break his neck, than that you should break his spirit.

—Robert Louis Stevenson

Dripping faucets, farts of passion, flat tires—are all sadder than death.

—Charles Bukowski

Kill Two Birds
& Get Stoned

CHAPTER 1

There are two good things about living in a basement apartment. The first is that you can't kill yourself by jumping out the window. The second, and this is an important one, is that whatever you do and wherever you go, you know you're always going to be on the way up. The bad thing, I suppose, is a matter of your point of view. All you ever see are people's feet walking by in the rain. Unless, of course, the sun is shining. You can't always tell, however, when you live in a basement apartment.

I suppose I ought to introduce myself. My name is Walter Snow and you probably never heard of me, which is not an especially good thing because I like to think of myself as a novelist. In fact, for the past few years I've been working on a project I half-tragically refer to as *The Great Armenian Novel*. I am not Armenian, though I once had an Armenian girlfriend, which at least qualifies me to write about what I know. Unfortunately, for years I hadn't written one word of the book. I suffered from writer's block. Or spiritual constipation. Or whatever you want to call it. And there is nothing worse in this or any other world than staring down at a blank piece of paper and realizing that it's as empty as your life.

All this, of course, was before I met Clyde Potts at the bank, and before she introduced me to Fox Harris. Even after all that has happened, I still think of both of them with a smile. I'm looking at that smile right now in the bathroom mirror. It looks a bit ragged, maybe a bit confused, but it's there all right. It lacks the innocence of a small boy at Christmas, and is probably a little closer to the sick, sweet, evil smile of the serial killer, redolent of charm and danger. But it is a fucking smile—and they say if you smile when you think of people who are gone, you loved them.

But let me redirect the conversation back to myself for a moment. I *am* a published novelist. Seven years ago I wrote a mildly successful, quirky little book about a man coming of age in a New Jersey nursing home. It was entitled *The Rise and Fall of Nothing at All* and its publication killed just enough trees to keep me in Camel filters and a basement apartment for seven years, which is saying something in today's market. But now I've moved from looking in the mirror to looking at the blank page again and I don't know which is worse. Both seem to somehow relate to those soulless attenuated feet that keep sliding silently by my window in the rain.

It's a dark and stormy day today and if you don't live in New York you might call it gloomy but if you do, you get used to it and a few other things. The only spot of color is provided by Fox's tropical fish, of which, I suppose, I am now the guardian. I don't know much about tropical fish except that bad things always seem to happen to their original owners. They're not too good for spiritually constipated novelists to have around either. They keep diverting your attention when you're busy staring at a blank page. But they're crazy and colorful, just like Fox: you never know what they're thinking, or if they're thinking. Also, they kind of hypnotize you if you look at them long enough. The bubbling sound takes a little while to get used to, but once you do, it blends right in with the sirens and the car alarms and the occasional junkie on the sidewalk shouting scripture. I haven't bonded with these fish, of course, and I don't think I'm likely to. But I intend to take good care of them. Sometimes late at night when I watch them swimming around in their aquarium I forget I'm in a basement apartment in New York City. At those times I think of the fish as little pieces of Fox's soul and the world seems like a bigger and brighter place. It almost feels good to be alive.

When I stop to reflect upon it, it was probably Fox and Clyde who deserve the credit, for better or worse, for knocking me off the wagon forever. Before that morning, when I first met Clyde at the bank, I'd had almost six and a half years of sobriety. I attended a secular rosary chain of AA meetings where I declared to the brainwashed and the unwashed of the world that my name was Walter and that I was an Alcoholic. My life had become an endless series of tableaus in which I would hold a Styrofoam cup of bad coffee—I never found out if the cup was half full or half empty—smoke an endless caravan of Camel filters and provide an ever-changing army of supportive strangers with my standard three minutes of superficial charm. If I had to talk to the same individual for much longer than three minutes, I could actually see the lines of ennui forming on his or her face and the undeniable presence of pity in his or her eyes. Speaking of his or her, I discovered that, as an alcoholic nondrinking nonwriting writer, I could extract more natural empathy from men than from women.

That, of course, was before I met Clyde at the bank.

I remember that morning surprisingly well, considering everything that's happened since. It was only about nine months ago but already it feels like two lifetimes interwoven like the careless arms of doomed lovers: the sweet, grievous lifetime of the saint mingling with the pregnant, existential lifetime of the sinner. And pregnant is the right word to use, for out of this dalliance have arisen three unique human entities, a trinity of bastard spirits destined never again to meet in this mortal world.

As I was saying, I think I was catching up on my masturbation that morning or maybe I was just standing by the window drinking a cup of good strong coffee from a real coffee mug, smoking a cigarette, watching feet pass me by in different directions, all going somewhere important, hurrying along into the cold and sun-splattered mosaic of the city. The morning was all kind of a blur until I left my apartment on Tenth Street and walked the few blocks through the Village to the small bank off Sheridan Square. I'd like to say I had a premonition of some sort, but it wouldn't be true. I was just another bank customer, trying to keep my balance. I was standing at one of those small tables they have, trying to reconcile meaningless numbers in my little bankbook, when I felt a presence from across the table. (There were no candles on the table, of course, but perhaps there should have been.) She had a gorgeous mass of golden storybook hair. She had a beauty mark on her right cheek. And when she took off her rather lavish sunglasses, she had the eyes of a slumming angel.

Her gaze lighted upon me with a graceful impudence that caused me to quickly look down at my bankbook. I have never thought of myself as a shy person. I think I'd just realized that one of those rare green flashes of insight that occur maybe once or twice in the lifetimes of the lucky was now taking place in a fucking bank. It was not love at first sight. That happens every day and usually results in a hostage situation. It was a far rarer, more sacred, more inherently animal experience than love often is. Here, I thought, for reasons yet unknown to me, stands a kindred spirit.

"Can you help me?" she asked, leaning forward conspiratorially across the little table that was the world. Our faces were suddenly very close together.

"I can do anything," I said, "except balance a bank account."

"I don't need an Einstein, Sunshine. Hey! That rhymes!"

"Yes. It does," I said nervously. The woman was obviously more than a little bit stoned, and yet she seemed in total control of herself, and me, for that matter. This could be quite dangerous. My name is Walter, I thought, and I'm an Alcoholic.

"My name is Walter," I said.

"I'm Clyde," she said, extending her hand in a surprisingly firm handshake. She was a tall, rawboned, sensuous-looking girl with an aura of country cool about her. At the time, I recall thinking that she was not quite beautiful. "Handsome" was the word that came to mind for her then. Now, of course, I realize she was beautiful. But then, a kindred spirit is bound to change your life. If you have a life.

"I've got something I need to keep in a safe-deposit box," she said, "but I don't have one and apparently there's a waiting list until the cows come home."

"That could be a long time in New York."

"I know," she said ruefully. "But you look

like the kind of person who might have a safe-deposit box."

As a child, I thought the last thing I wanted to do was to grow up and look like the kind of person who had a safe-deposit box. I wanted to be Robin Hood or Jesse James, the kind of people who dedicated their lives to robbing safe-deposit boxes. I never in my wildest childhood dreams believed I'd be the kind of person who could be defeated daily by a blank page or the sort who'd stand around holding a Styrofoam cup baring his human soul to an army of the ambulatory wounded. Unfortunately, I did have a safe-deposit box. And do you know what was in it? Nothing. That, I reflected briefly, was perhaps worse than having one in the first place.

"As it happens, I do have a safe-deposit box," I said.

"Yippee!" she said, a little too loudly for inside the bank, I thought. "Let's go."

"Not so fast," I said. "Just what are we putting in my safe-deposit box?"

"Oh, it's nothing illegal," said Clyde. "It's my grandmother's heirloom silverware set from Russia. She was a Gypsy and she carried it with her all over Russia and then gave it to my mother who lives in South Dakota and she sent it to me because she's afraid her boyfriend might steal it."

"Why would her boyfriend steal it?"

"He's a Gypsy."

"I see."

"No, you don't really. Nobody ever does. I

7

think that's the main problem with this whole damn town."

"And I always thought it was finding a parking place."

"I don't have a car," she said. "And I don't have a damn safe-deposit box and I'm afraid Fox will steal my grandmother's silverware and sell it to buy drugs or something."

"Who's Fox?"

"He's the king of the Gypsies. He's also my roommate. I'd trust him with my life but not my grandmother's silverware. Now can I store this stuff in your box or not? Remember, I'll have to trust you at least as much as you have to trust me."

And so we did.

The bank officer walked the two of us into the vault like any conventional little married couple. Then, with his master key and my key he unlocked the two locks on the box and discreetly left the room. Clyde extracted a wrapped parcel from the large purse she was carrying. She had her sunglasses back on but I didn't think anything of it at the time. She handed me the package and I dutifully placed it into my empty little safe-deposit box.

"Thanks," murmured Clyde, dangerously close to my right ear. "I know Granny's silver will be safe now."

I was beginning to have a few second thoughts by this time, but I didn't let them go anywhere.

8

For one thing, Clyde did have to trust me as much as I had to trust her. If the contents of the box were anything other than her grandmother's heirloom silverware, she would still require my help to ever gain its possession again. I, on the other hand, had to take her at her word. If this was some kind of con, it was certainly a strange one.

The bank officer took the master key and the box and filed it away in its secure little cranny and the girl and I left the vault and walked out into the sunny chill of the city. On the back of a bank-deposit slip Clyde wrote her name and phone number. I gave her my card. It'd been a while since I'd given anyone my card and I needed the practice. She put the card in her purse and then leaned over and kissed me softly on the lips. She'd get in touch soon, she said. I watched her for a long time as she walked down the street and finally disappeared into the subway.

You've got to trust somebody sometime, I figured. The whole world isn't always out to screw you. That's what I thought at the time. That was, of course, before I started collecting tropical fish. Bad things seem to happen to people who collect tropical fish.

CHAPTER 2

It must have been about two weeks after that when the cops showed up at my door. To be technically correct, they did not show up at my door. They rapped on the window of my basement apartment. That's another bad feature I forgot to mention. When you live in a basement apartment, sometimes you look up from toasting your bagel and you see a cop standing next to a trash can, rapping on your window with a night-stick that wants to be a Louisville Slugger when it grows up. The cop is crouching by the window and he has a clear view of everything going on in your apartment. Fortunately, he only catches you toasting a bagel. Imagine if he'd discovered you a few moments before involved in a more provocative pastime such as self-gratification or smoking dope or, God help us all, writing.

I saw one cop gesturing to me from between the garbage cans, toward the front door of the building. At that time in my life, I was not very paranoid and in fact had nothing at all to hide, so I buzzed the cops into the building. The two of them clumped around in the hallway for a minute and then I opened the door and they popped up about the same time the bagels did. I took this as a good sign. For one thing, it was the first time the toaster had worked in weeks without burning the bagels and making the apartment look like the pope had just died. For another, it was the first time anybody'd come to visit me for a while. I'd never in my life been visited by cops. I couldn't imagine what they wanted.

Two cops and a novelist with writer's block can pretty well take up most of the space in a small basement apartment. That was before the fish tank, but it was still a tad bit claustrophobic. They established that I was, indeed, Walter Snow, but they didn't seem in any particular hurry to get down to business.

"Nice place you have here," said one of the cops. He was a thin, hatchet-faced man whose name appeared to be Roth.

"Ain't every window in New York," said the other one, "where you get a view lookin' up at garbage cans." He chuckled a bit and had a fairly large gut and his name was Shelby.

"Everybody finds their own level," said Roth. He didn't chuckle. He didn't seem to be the chuckling type.

"Well, what can I help you with, officers?" I said.

"'What can I help you with, officers?'" mimicked Shelby. "That's a good one."

"How about we ask the questions," said Roth, with a sneer of disgust.

11

I was truly mystified. I couldn't get the bagels out of the toaster and I couldn't get the cops out of the apartment and I couldn't figure out what the hell they were there for in the first place. I was starting to feel a bit like Franz Kafka but then I remembered I had writer's block.

"What do you do for a living, Mr. Snow?" Shelby was asking. Roth took a quick glance into the dumper and came up with another sneer of disgust. There wasn't really anything wrong with the dumper except it was just about the size of a small pantry closet.

"I'm a novelist," I said.

"A novelist?" said Roth, making a little show of gazing around the place as if it were a large, luxurious apartment.

"Well," I said, "I haven't really written anything in almost seven years."

Shelby nodded his head sagely. "And why would that be, Mr. Snow?"

"I wish I knew the answer to that one," I said, with what was getting to be a practiced ruefulness. "I just don't seem to be able to write anymore."

"Shame," said Roth.

"Lot of talent gone to waste," offered Shelby with a strange smile.

"That's what my aunt Beatrice always told me," I said.

"She live in the city?" asked Shelby.

"No," I answered. "She's dead."

"Shame," said Roth.

I hadn't had much experience with cops, as I said, but it seemed to me that they were interviewing me as if I was not the law-abiding citizen I knew I was. I was racking my brains trying to figure out what they were doing here in the first place.

"Look, officers," I said after a long period of strained silence, "would you mind telling me what you want from me?"

"Oh, I think you probably do know the answer to that one," said Shelby. He was chuckling again but I could see that it was just kind of an ingrained habit, like a nervous tic or something. He wasn't really getting much amusement out of the situation. Of course, neither was I.

"Still can't guess?" said Roth, like a facetious, rather cynical game-show host.

Alarm bells were now going off somewhere in the deep recesses of my mind. Somewhere in there as well was probably a full-length novel yet to be written. But I didn't have the novel and I didn't have the answer. I tried to think of anything I'd done recently that had been unusual or out of character for me. Suddenly, it hit me. I've never been much of a poker player and I guess the cops could tell.

"That's right," nodded Shelby. "It's the bank, stupid."

"The bank?" I said. But I knew he was right. It was the bank. It was the safe-deposit box. It was helping Clyde stash her grandmother's silverware.

I'd wondered about what was in the parcel at the time but was too shy or too weak or too stupid to make her unwrap it. Now two cops were crowding me out of my basement apartment. I lit a cigarette. I offered the pack to the cops but they declined.

I walked a few steps to the kitchen area and poured myself a cup of coffee with a slightly shaky hand. I offered the two cops some coffee. They declined again with an almost fatalistic patience that I found rather unnerving.

"Why'd you do it?" asked Roth.

"I was just trying to help that woman named Clyde. I didn't know what was in the package. I thought it was her grandmother's silverware."

"Her grandmother's silverware?" said Roth incredulously.

"A woman named Clyde?" said Shelby.

"What's her last name?" asked Roth.

"Potts. But I—"

"Have you talked to her since you—ah—helped her in the bank?" asked Shelby.

"I tried to call her last week but the number she gave me has been disconnected."

"Shame," said Roth.

I killed the cigarette and went over slowly to pour another cup of coffee. I tried to think. What in the hell was going on here?

"Look, guys," I said finally, "why won't you tell me what's happening? Who's Clyde? What did you find in my safe-deposit box?"

"We didn't find anything," said Shelby. "The

bank found something and it wasn't her grandmother's silverware. First, of course, they had to get a court order and then they had to drill the box open. You won't be banking there anymore but I'm sure they'll be getting in touch with you. They could've filed criminal charges but since this broad has done this before in other banks with other marks like yourself, they'll probably let you off. Same reason we're not going to haul you in today for criminal mischief and maybe a felony or two if we wanted to try real hard."

"In other words," said Roth, apparently observing my total lack of understanding as to what had occurred, "you've been duped, Mr. Snow. But don't feel too bad about it. There's a sucker born every minute, and here in New York it's a regular population explosion. People like this Clyde woman eat people like you for breakfast every morning, and by lunchtime, they're hungry again. Fortunately, there's plenty of suckers like you around. I doubt if she'll bother with you again though. If she does get in touch, of course, you will call us?"

"Of course," I said.

The cops were making moves to leave by now and I was truly beginning to feel like the idiot they thought I was. They'd put me through the Chinese water torture and I still didn't know what Clyde had conned me into. I knew what I'd been. A sucker. I just didn't know how or why. That's enough to make even a sucker mad.

"Wait a minute!" I said with some intensity. "You can't leave without telling me what it was that the bank found in my safe-deposit box. What was it? Drugs? Stolen money?"

"Worse," said Roth. "A dead fish."

Many hours later, sometime after midnight in fact, I was lying half awake in bed imagining a scene in a novel about two police detectives interrogating a man in a basement apartment. The cops were ruthless and persistent. The man didn't have the vaguest notion what they wanted him for. The walls were closing in on the man. Then the phone rang.

The scene disappeared somewhere in my head but the phone was still ringing. The alarm clock read 12:55. I got out of bed, walked over to my desk, and picked up the phone.

"Hello, Sunshine."

"Clyde?"

"The one and only. Sorry I haven't called you. Do you want to have lunch with me tomorrow at the Blue Mill? Tomorrow's my birthday."

"Happy birthday, Clyde."

"Thanks, honey."

"Clyde, why'd you do it?"

"Do what?"

"Why'd you put the dead fish in my safe-deposit box?"

There was a silence on the line. It wasn't really a silence because I could hear the noise of the street all around her, and she stood in my mind like a beautiful spiritual tramp at a pay phone somewhere with cars and laughter and street orators, headlights and sirens all around her. In my imagination, she was the most seductive siren of them all. She'd make a great character in a novel, I thought. I'm not going to tell the cops she called, I thought.

"Okay. I'll tell you why I did it if you promise not to be mad, Sunshine."

"All right. I promise."

"I did it just for the halibut," she said.

After she'd hung up, I went back to bed and, for the first time in what seemed like a thousand years, I think I went to sleep with a smile on my face.

CHAPTER 3

"So, what do you know, Walter Snow?" she said, making it rhyme, leaning back in the booth. We were at the Blue Mill on Barrow Street and the lunch crowd seemed pretty light. It looked like it might be a fairly intimate birthday party.

"You look great, Clyde," I said. "But you sure don't look like the girl I met at the bank."

"Of course not, honey. I lost the wig, lost the Holly Golightly sunglasses, and even lost the beauty mark on my cheek. Remember?"

"Oh, I remember. I bet the security cameras at the bank remember, too."

"Well, you know how it is. A girl can't be too careful these days."

"I'll never tell the cops," I said. "You can count on me."

"I do, Sunshine."

It was incredible how fast I was becoming accustomed to the new Clyde. Or maybe it was the old Clyde. Anyway, the eyes still had it. They shone with an animal-like sense of excitement and a childlike spirit of mischief. If I had known better,

18

I'd have said they were pulling me into her world. And she somehow looked smaller and more feminine now. Blond hair cut short with punkish pink highlights. That same indecipherable, seductively crooked smile. It was enough to make me want to follow her gorgeous ass into battle as if she were some jaded Joan of Arc. It was almost enough to make me want to write.

"The fish was fun, though, wasn't it?" she said. "You *knew* it wasn't my grandmother's heirloom silverware, didn't you?"

"Sort of," I said. "Maybe I was just mesmerized by your beauty mark. I kind of miss it."

"Don't worry. I'm liable to bring it back at any time. I wonder where Fox is. He's supposed to be baking and bringing my birthday cake."

"Your friend Fox knows how to bake a birthday cake?"

"He's a man of many talents," said Clyde. "While we're waiting, what do you say to a little after-dinner drink?"

"Fine. What would you like?"

"Tequila," said Clyde. "In fact, *tres* tequilas."

"*Tres* tequilas?"

"That's right, Sunshine. Guaranteed to keep away the blues at birthday time!"

Three tequilas in the middle of the afternoon was not a policy usually prescribed by the people who frequently attended AA meetings. If those kind of people ever downed three tequilas, they might well wind up doing something really crazy. Like putting

19

a dead fish in a bank vault. I signaled the waiter and explained the order, which was now six tequilas because after some thought I decided I wasn't going to let Clyde drink alone on her birthday. As the waiter walked away, I saw Clyde studying me. It was a surprisingly pleasant sensation.

"This may be a rude question," she said, "but what is it you do when you're not busy playing Sir Lancelot coming to the aid of dangerous, deceiving women whom you think are damsels in distress?"

"That's not a rude question," I said, "just a hard one."

"Let me see if I can guess the answer. All I really know about you is that you're a good sport, you have a trusting nature, and you're a gentle, kind spirit who wouldn't let a girl celebrate her birthday all by herself. How's that for a start?"

"I'm starting to like myself already."

The waiter came to the table with a tray upon which sat six healthy shots of tequila along with a saucer of salt and some slices of lime. The Blue Mill was a fairly quiet, sedate kind of place and not a few other patrons raised a tentative eyebrow upon observing six drinks being delivered to a party of two. I told the waiter to put the meals and the drinks on one check and to keep the tab open.

"I forgot to mention 'big spender,'" said Clyde, smiling approvingly. "You sure I can't help you foot the bill?"

"On your birthday? Not a chance."

"So you're not an accountant," said Clyde. "You're too easy with your money and you haven't even mentioned the receipt."

"Right."

"You're not a doctor or a lawyer or a shrink. You don't dress the part, and besides, you're too loose and easy with your time. I doubt if any of them would have *tres* tequilas in the middle of a workday. Of course, you never know."

"No. You're right. I'm none of the above."

"Let's drink to none of the above," said Clyde, lifting her glass.

And we did.

"All right," said Clyde. "I'd like to keep guessing what you're not and maybe what you are. Is the game getting boring?"

"Nothing about you could ever be boring."

"Oh, God! Don't tell me you're a professional escort! A gigolo! No, I've got it! A male prostitute! No, that can't be. You wouldn't be picking up the tab."

"You're right."

"Besides, you're not *that* charming. Just kidding. Well, let's see. What's left? You're not a teacher. You couldn't afford the drinks."

"Right."

"And speaking of drinks, how about another round? Where the hell's my birthday cake? I knew I shouldn't have trusted Fox. Birthdays can be such a drag anyway and then to have a birthday party and no cake—"

"This is the best birthday party I've ever been to in my life," I said truthfully.

"*Sure* you're not a professional escort?"

"Positive."

"Well," she said, lifting a second tequila high in the air, "here's to amateurs."

We drank the second shot of tequila. By this time, I wasn't sure if it was the tequila or simply being with Clyde that was creating the current state of near happiness that I was feeling. I found myself hoping that her friend Fox would be a no-show.

"You're not self-absorbed enough to be a college professor. Your hands are too soft and clean to be a punch-press operator. You're too sweet to be a cop. Too smart to be a drug dealer. Too innocent to be a reporter. And we know you're not a banker or you never would've let me use your safe-deposit box in the first place and—we wouldn't be here together now."

"Right on all counts. I'm again none of the above."

Clyde folded her hands and rested her chin on her fingers. She looked past my eyes into my dreams.

"What manner of man are you, Sunshine?" she asked, her demeanor suddenly transformed to that of a curious, highly intelligent child.

She was a woman. She was a con artist. She was a chameleon. And what manner of man was I? That might have been an even harder question. For it's easy to lie to yourself, but it's not so easy to lie to a child. And now, for all the world, she looked at me with the eyes of a child.

"I'm a writer," I said. "But I don't write. I mean, I used to write but that was years ago. If I was writing now, I'd be writing a novel. I'm a novelist, I suppose. I write fiction."

"My life is a work of fiction," she said. "I love fiction. It's always so true."

I looked up and the child was gone. In her place there was a beautiful woman. She was holding a glass and making a toast.

"Here's to the big new best-seller by Walter Snow!" she said.

"I'll drink to that," I said.

"You'll write it, too," said Clyde.

What happened next is a little difficult to remember. *Tres* tequilas will do that to you. And we didn't stop at three. Fox Harris came whirling into the place with an entrance quite theatrical, carrying a large cardboard box very delicately, dressed in a flowing blue robe, and strutting past the stares, both cold and curious, of the assembled patrons like a proud and handsome king, which in many ways he was. Or maybe I should say queen. I wasn't sure then and I'm not entirely certain now. I'm not even sure that it makes any difference.

As Fox approached our table, with his long, unkempt locks of hair flowing in every possible direction, he began singing quite loudly to the bemusement or studied indifference of the other customers and to the perfect joy of Clyde.

"'MacArthur's Park is melting in the dark, all that sweet green icing oozing down,'" he paraphrased as he discarded the box on the floor, revealing a beautiful chocolate cake that he danced around displaying to the patrons, many of whom appeared as if they'd been hit by a hammer. Now he sang louder and more emotionally, playing to his audience like a torch singer.

"Someone left the cake out in the rain,
I don't know if I can make it,
It took so long to bake it,
And I'll never have that recipe again!"

He came over to our table then, placed the cake precariously atop a small platform of the six empty tequila glasses, and gave Clyde a long hug, which at moments seemed brotherly, at others seemed motherly, and still at others seemed loverly. I was mildly surprised to notice a small but definite streak of jealousy manifesting itself in my heart. I hardly knew these people, I recall thinking at the time. I realize now, of course, that I hardly knew myself.

"Welcome to the caravan, Walter," he said at last, winking broadly at Clyde. "I've heard a lot about you."

He extended a firm hand from somewhere within the bountiful folds of his royal blue robe. I shook hands with the man Clyde had called the king of the Gypsies and, indeed, his eyes seemed to sparkle with life and love and destiny like the slow-moving spokes of a Gypsy wagon. He gazed down at the table and his face suddenly registered great shock.

"Don't tell me," he shouted, "that you both have had *tres* tequilas without me!"

"You were late, Fox," said Clyde. "You're always late."

"That's an occupational hazard," he said, "of a homeless man without subway fare. Thank God Walter's here. Bartender! Nine more tequilas! What do you two think of the cake?"

"Looks yummy," said Clyde.

"Baked it myself. German chocolate. Do you know the recipe, Walter, for German chocolate cake?"

"I'm afraid I don't," I said.

"Well, the first step is, you occupy the kitchen."

This drew a mild guffaw from the large, rather portly waiter who proceeded to deposit nine more tequilas on the table. Clyde, Fox, and I proceeded to kill the first round and I thought for a while that I could actually keep up with them. Clyde clearly could drink like a fish, and I don't mean the one that smelled up the bank. Fox's basic demeanor was so ebullient and mercurial it had been hard to tell if he was drunk or sober from the moment he'd walked into the place. Maybe he was dead drunk. Maybe he merely seemed to appear increasingly more dignified. Maybe, as Fox contended later, there was very little difference between those two states of human behavior.

By the fifth round of tequila, I was having a little trouble focusing my eyes but I could make out Fox Harris jumping around like a spinning ghost and striking a kitchen match on his jeans.

"Make a wish," he shouted, lighting the single huge candle on the cake, which he later confided he'd stolen from the Church of the Latter Day Felcher. Clyde closed her eyes, and with a particularly dreamy expression on her face, made a wish.

"What'd you wish for?" asked Fox.

"I'm not telling," said Clyde. "Anyway, it's not about you. It's about Walter."

"Then it's about me, too," Fox persisted, raising his voice in righteous passion. "We're all part of one big soul! It's one for all! All for one!"

"That's true," Clyde said wistfully. "But I was wishing for something that only Walter can do."

"Write the bloody novel?" I asked.

"You'll write the novel when you're ready to write the novel," she said. "I'm wishing for something even more important. Maybe I'll tell you someday."

"I'll tell you one thing," said Fox. "You better blow that fucking candle out before the whole cake turns into a wax museum."

Clyde puckered her lips very suggestively, I thought, and smoothly blew out the candle to a loud cheer from Fox and light applause from myself and the waiter, who appeared to be standing by nervously with the check. I gave him my credit card and he walked away just as Fox pulled out what appeared to be a hunting knife from the medieval-looking scabbard hooked on his braided belt. He was moving to cut the cake when Clyde leaped up to stop him.

"Put that dirty, ugly thing away," she said. "This is a nohands birthday cake. You can't touch it with your hands or a knife or a fork—only your mouth."

"Can we use your grandmother's heirloom silverware?" I asked.

"The boy's good," said Fox.

"Only your *mouth*," said Clyde.

As monstered on tequila as I was at the time, as blurry as everything else seems in retrospect, what occurred in the next few minutes remains indelibly and finely etched in my memory. Clyde was the first to take a bite out of the cake. Then Fox took a large mouthful. Then, incredibly, I began eating the large chocolate birthday cake with only my mouth, to the horror of the remaining diners at the placid, traditional old Blue Mill. Soon all three of us were devouring Fox Harris's culinary masterpiece like a pack of hyenas. The chocolate cake was all over our faces, the waiter was standing by stoically, and the two bartenders were conferring darkly behind the bar.

It was at this point that Fox began putting cake in Clyde's hair. Clyde responded by putting cake in Fox's hair, though with Fox's hair it was not that noticeable. Then they both began putting cake in my hair, as well as licking some of the chocolate icing off each other's faces. Then Clyde came over closer to me and set about seductively licking my face. Then, as the waiter finally brought the credit-card receipt for me to sign, I became vaguely aware that my forward progress was being impeded by the unnatural act of Fox Harris licking my reading glasses.

At this juncture, a no-nonsense management type dressed in a conservative suit walked briskly across the room to put an end to the insanity. That this did not occur immediately is probably a tribute to Clyde's inherent ability to charm any snake in the universe, particularly the two-legged male variety. She turned to face the manager just as he approached the table and with great dignity brushed back a bit of cake-ravaged hair, looked into his eyes, smiled shyly, and stuck out her hand as if he'd asked her to dance.

In the twinkle of an eye, they formed a tableau of two old smoothy sweethearts on the dance floor. Fox was suddenly beside them clapping his hands in waltz time and crooning along encouragingly.

"'Two drifters,'" sang Fox, "'off to see the world. There's such a lot of world to see. We're after the same rainbow's end—'"

Now Fox was whirling around with some invisible partner, twirling his robe exaggeratively, keeping the music going. And the manager was dancing with Clyde.

"'—my huckleberry friend,'" Fox sang. "'Moon Riv-er-and me.'"

When Fox had run out of lyrics, he came over and stood beside me. Clyde and the manager continued to dance silently for a moment or two, the manager struggling vainly to conceal a slightly confused and bright-eyed smile. Clyde's face looked positively angelic.

"Want to hear something really funny?" said Fox. "It's not even her birthday."

CHAPTER 4

I had a hangover the next day but also a rather strange and happy afterglow. There had been something about that Mad Hatter Tea Party atmosphere surrounding the worlds of Clyde Potts and Fox Harris that threatened to draw me into their orbit, into a universe that I suspected might be quite different from my own. I didn't know where they lived, if they lived together, what exactly their relationship was, what they did, or who they really were. I just knew that I liked them and maybe a little bit more. All I had to show for knowing them at all was a letter from the bank coldly critiquing the kind of person I was, threatening my firstborn, and closing out my account. And a hangover. And, of course, the rather strange and happy afterglow. It seemed like a pretty good deal at the time.

I didn't hear from Clyde for several days. Indeed, I was beginning to wonder if I'd ever hear from her again. Then, on the third day, just as I was manhandling my recalcitrant toaster, the phone rang. I walked over to my desk, nervously lit a cigarette, and picked up the receiver.

"Sunshine?"

I was relieved to hear that voice.

"Yes."

"Are you all right?"

"Now I am."

"Good. I'm calling a meeting of the Three Musketeers tonight at seven-thirty. Will you be there?"

I said I would and she gave me an address in midtown and told me to meet her and Fox on the street outside. I said I would. She hung up before I could say anything else. If the truth be told, I wouldn't have missed it for the world. Clyde and Fox seemed to be the two liveliest people I'd ever met in my life. That seemed like a pretty good reason then. Even now, it doesn't seem like a bad one.

It was balefully obvious to me by this time, of course, that I'd taken a fairly severe tumble off the old AA wagon. Beware the company you keep, my mother always told me, and she wasn't wrong. But sometimes the company you keep keeps you. Sometimes the company you keep keeps *you* from being a sheep. I smoked Camel filters that afternoon, drank coffee, and gave up on the toaster. I was unsure how many tequilas I'd drunk three days before because Fox had no proprietary sense at all and had drunk some of mine. I'd drunk enough, however, to remind me that, in a battle with a toaster, man will always lose. A little alcohol in the system will occasionally give you new insights. Now I realized that man cannot live on bagels alone. So I went out for lunch.

At a little before seven, I took a cab uptown, found the address Clyde had given me, and waited around on the sidewalk. It was Friday evening and people were rushing to get home or to the bars or to wherever they go. I had forgotten that people went out in the evening. The whole scene was vaguely reminiscent of a recently agitated ant colony. About the only people in New York who weren't there were Clyde and Fox. I took out a cigarette, lit it up, paced the sidewalk a bit, and waited. By seven forty-five, I was beginning to wonder if the two of them were up to something that did not include me. Again I felt the unwelcome, irrational stirrings of jealousy, which I knew was crazy and self-defeating. As Fox would tell me later, "Jealousy is not always unfounded or irrational. It's just possible that everybody *is* better than you."

Two cigarettes later, a few minutes after eight o'clock, they both came walking up the sidewalk together, laughing. Clyde came up to me immediately and gave me a light kiss on the lips followed by a warm and lingering hug. Fox, I noticed, was wearing the same royal blue robes but at least he'd changed his pants. The pair he was wearing now looked like a hand-me-down from Professor Harold Hill in *The Music Man* but it was cleaner than what he'd worn earlier in the week. Not that I was a clothing maven of any kind but the last pair he'd worn had revealed a little more of Fox than anybody wanted to see. Clyde was dressed rather seductively in a tight black-leather outfit that made her look like a biker chick in a very upscale gang. For myself, I suppose I looked casual but well turned out, like a novelist who wasn't writing but still dressed the part.

You may wonder why I'm nattering on about sartorial matters. It's just something I learned from Clyde Potts. "What you wear is of very little concern. How you wear what you wear is everything." Fox and I may have made a few mistakes in our time, but in my experience with Clyde, I've never known her to be wrong. Except possibly, of course, about me and Fox.

"Sorry we're late, Sunshine," she said lightly. "It was all Fox's fault."

"Don't try to shift the blame to me," he said. "It was all your fault."

"When are you ever going to learn," asked Clyde, "to take responsibility for your own actions?"

"Only a madman would take responsibility for my actions," said Fox indignantly.

"You're right, darling," said Clyde. "And that's why we love you. Don't we, Sunshine?"

Fox appeared to be staring at me expectantly, like a small child waiting for his mother's approval. I didn't exactly love Fox back then, but in time, incredibly perhaps, even that would change.

"Of course," I answered generously. "By the way, don't tell me we're going to Bennigan's?"

"Careful what you say about Bennigan's," warned Clyde. "It's one of Fox's favorite places."

"I don't believe it," I said. "Fox likes Bennigan's?"

"Judge ye not," Fox intoned, "lest ye be a tourist from Kansas. It is true that I have little in common with the chain people who've made Bennigan's one of our country's most popular chain restaurants. But the chain people and I like Bennigan's for *very* different reasons. As you shall soon see."

But before I could see what Fox was yapping about, I saw something else. I saw Clyde move very close to me and hook her trim arm around mine. It made my arm feel warm all over. Then I saw Fox lock elbows with Clyde on the other side and suddenly the two of them were skipping down the sidewalks of New York dragging me along with them and singing, "'We're off to see the wizard—the wonderful Wizard of Oz!'" I wasn't sure if I was meant to be the Tin Man, the Scarecrow, the Cowardly Lion—or Dorothy. It was one thing to drink an ungodly number of tequilas and help devour a no-hands birthday cake in a half-empty restaurant. But it was quite another to be stone-cold sober and frolicking like a young schoolgirl before the jaded, judgmental eyes of a crowded block full of New Yorkers. I knew, of course, that New Yorkers had seen just about everything, but I didn't really feel as if they needed to see this particular spectacle at this time. And there was no gracious way to stop the event until Clyde or Fox ran out of energy, and the two of them appeared to be in some kind of competition to see who could keep going the longest. I felt like a shy young boy taking his first dance lessons. When the ordeal was over at last, we'd passed Bennigan's by a good two and a half blocks.

"That's my aerobics for the week," said Fox. "Got a cigarette?" I gave him a cigarette.

"Me, too, Sunshine," said Clyde. I gave her a cigarette.

"Got a light?" asked Fox. I took out my lighter and lit his cigarette.

"Me, too, Sunshine," said Clyde. As I lit her cigarette, she cupped her hand around mine and stared directly into my eyes. When the cigarette was lit, she tapped my hand once gently with her index finger. Then she winked a beautiful wink I will never forget. As an author, even one with spiritual constipation, you may well expect me to be able to describe that wink. Unfortunately, I've never been very good at describing winks. But this one sailed as silver and simple as a hummingbird at dawn or a bullet to the heart.

"Okay," I said. "Where do we go now?"

"Back to Bennigan's, of course," said Fox. "What would cause you to think otherwise?"

"Don't try to follow Fox's logic," said Clyde. "He doesn't have any."

"You don't need logic," said Fox, "once you successfully mistake your own sick fantasy for wisdom."

"See what I mean?" said Clyde. Then she took

us both firmly by the arm, and this time, calmly and leisurely, we all walked back to Bennigan's.

If anything, the sidewalks seemed to be even more crowded now, and when we approached the entrance to Bennigan's, I could see that it was fairly swarming with the clientele Fox liked to refer to as "the chain people." I wasn't sure if Fox included me in this unfortunate grouping or not. I like to think my spiritual stature grew in his eyes over the time we were together but I never really summoned the courage to ask him.

"Ah, the teeming masses," said Fox, flicking his cigarette into the gutter, "yearning to breathe smoke free." Smoking was allowed at the bar and the little tables in the vicinity of the bar and this was the area in which we were told by Fox to reconnoiter. He made sure that we staggered our entrances with an almost military precision.

Clyde went first, then me, then Fox, at intervals of several minutes. At last, we rejoined Clyde at a small high table without chairs near the bar surrounded by a sea of chain people.

"Do we know each other?" I asked, only half facetiously.

"The human soul is unknowable," said Fox. "You got a hundred-dollar bill?"

"I'm not sure," I said. "Why?"

"Give it to me," said Fox.

I cast a quizzical eye at Clyde but she had on her world-class poker face. It told you nothing but made you want everything.

"Do what the man says," she said.

I took out my billfold, found a hundred-dollar bill, and handed it to Fox. It sounded like some kind of shakedown, I'll admit, but it felt all right because I trusted Clyde. Strange as it may seem, I trusted the woman who'd talked me into permitting her to put a dead fish in my safe-deposit box. Would I walk through the Valley of the Shadow of Death for this woman? I wondered. At that moment, it appeared to be an open question.

I handed the hundred-dollar bill to Fox, who snapped it once between his finger and his thumb and then gave it to Clyde. Clyde took the bill and put it facedown on the table in front of her.

"Got a pen, Sunshine?" she asked sweetly.

"Of course he does," said Fox. "Every big best-selling novelist carries a pen. It's their weapon of choice."

"Don't let Fox get under your skin," said Clyde. "He's just testing you."

"He's doing a pretty good job," I said. I handed the pen to Clyde.

"Go with the social security number," said Fox. "That always plays well."

Clyde began marking her numbers down on the back of the bill. When she'd completed the little task, she gave the bill back to Fox. He gave it back to me.

"Put it back in your wallet," he said.

I put the bill in my wallet. "What happens now?" I asked.

"Now it's your turn, Walter," said Fox.

"Why me?" I asked, trying to mask an incipient state of mild nervousness. "Whatever it is we're doing, it looks like you both have done it before."

"That's why it's your turn," said Fox.

"And you're right, Walter," said Clyde seriously. "We have both done this before. We've done it countless times before. But each time we do it, it's an adventure all its own."

"Anyway," said Fox, "you've got the easy part. All you have to do is go up to the bar, order us all a round of drinks, and pay the bartender with that marked C-note."

"I think I can handle it," I said. "Is there a name for this particular exercise?"

"Well, the cops call it something else," said Fox. "I like to call it the ol' switcheroo. It's just a little thing I learned when I lived with the Gypsies. It helps keep you on your toes. Lets you know you're alive. It also is not without some practical applications. You'll see. Now go order the drinks."

They were both drinking scotch that night, so I decided to go along with them and keep us all on a Chivas Regal wavelength, realizing that it was to be my first Chivas in almost seven years. I ordered doubles from the bartender, figuring whatever we were about to do might go off a little more smoothly if we all had a little buzz going. When I got to know Fox and Clyde a bit better, I realized that I needn't have been concerned. They needed no artificial stimulation of any kind. They always had a little buzz going.

I paid the much-harassed bartender with the designated bill, received the change, and took the drinks back to the table.

"My name is Walter," I said as I placed the drinks in front of them. "I'll be your server this evening."

"Out of the mouths of babes," said Clyde.

"Great job, Walter," said Fox. "Phase one is now complete."

"What's phase two?" I asked.

Fox took a healthy sip from his glass. "Phase two is we drink the scotch," he said.

Clyde's face had softened and now she looked at me warmly. Her eyes were still impossible to read, but at least she seemed to be acknowledging what I believed to be a growing friendship between us.

"Phase two is my favorite part," she said, sipping the scotch. "Except for phase three, of course. It just keeps getting better."

"That's the whole point of living," said Fox.

"I liked the way you handled yourself, Sunshine," she said. "You could be really good someday."

"At what?" I asked, still fairly mystified about the whole scenario.

"Ah," said Fox. "That's the question."

If that was the question, apparently there was not going to be any immedaite answer. Fox and Clyde each bummed a cigarette and the three of us smoked and drank in silence for a time. All around us moved a rolling ocean of gray, oblivious, practically interchangeable mortal units that I did not know and that I did not really want to know. Whatever native sensitivity I had told me in no uncertain terms that I was with two of the most colorful, exciting, soulful people in the world that night and that this was only the beginning of my journey. I do not think I was wrong in my assessment of the situation. If I made a mistake, it was to err on the side of being human. And, as Fox often pointed out, to err on the side of being human is never a mistake.

"This is so nice," said Clyde. "I haven't felt this close to anybody in such a peaceful way since I was a little girl under the comforter in my mother's bed during a terrible thunderstorm with my older brother John and my dog Toulouse. It felt so safe and warm and right. Through all the storms and travels and adventures when I was a kid—and I'm still a kid—I was always thinking back to that moment and I knew I was at home base."

"Home plate," said Fox, not unkindly.

"I was a girl," said Clyde. "To me it was home base."

"Where was your mother during the storm?" I asked.

"My mother was a hooker, Walter," said Clyde. "But she provided for John, Toulouse, and me. John died on a hill in Vietnam. Toulouse died in a kitchen in Miami after he licked the floor following a visit by the exterminator. I don't know where my mother died. Probably in a thousand cheap motel rooms. That's why everybody needs a home base."

Clyde killed her cigarette and stared empty eyed into some middle distance. I looked down at my scotch and didn't say a thing. Fox, quite out of tune with the rather somber moment, began to dance wildly around the little table.

"But you're here now!" he shouted amidst the din. "And Walter's here now! And I'm here now! I want to be part of it! New York, New York! I want to live! I want to paint!"

"Hush," said Clyde, grabbing his arm and yanking him back to his place at the table. "You'll blow phase three."

"Sorry," said Fox meekly.

"Fox gets carried away sometimes," Clyde explained. "Sometimes they carry him away."

I nodded my head and took it all in as if it made sense. And in a sense, I suppose, it did. We live in a crazy world, and if you want to get through it with your body and soul even a little bit intact, you might as well be crazy yourself. It couldn't hurt. And it just might help.

"Okay," said Fox, his eyes suddenly shining like two light-houses. "It's time for the ol' switcheroo. Are you ready, Ms. Potts?"

"I've been ready all my life," she said.

I sensed a rekindled spirit in both of them that was almost palpable. And the excitement was infectious. Almost magically I felt invisible energy fields forming around our little table in the crowded room. In an environment numbed and deadened by convention, conformity, and confusion, a life force that I could not understand appeared to be focusing upon my very being. Perhaps it was ridiculous. Perhaps it was my imagination. Perhaps it was just that these extremely vibrant, fun-loving, alive people were embarking upon an adventure and I was a part of it. I realize now, of course, that that was a highly romanticized, deeply naive, and alcohol-induced view of things, but if two people can put back into you what a lifetime has tried to beat out of you, maybe it really happened like I imagined and, what's more, maybe it was all worthwhile.

"Wish me luck," said Clyde, her very countenance aglow.

"Wait a minute," said Fox. "We've forgotten something important. Possibly vital."

"What?" I said, before I could stop myself. Not only did I have no clue as to what they were doing, but I also had no idea what Fox was nattering on about.

It didn't take long for me to find out. Before I knew it, Fox had slipped his little finger around my little finger with an intensity that was almost painful. Across the table, he'd done the same thing with Clyde. Smiling indulgently, she reached across to perform the same inane maneuver with my other hand, thereby completing the little circle of madness.

"Lock pinkies!" shouted Fox.

"Just humor him," Clyde advised me. "He does have his moments. Unfortunately, this isn't one of them."

With that, she disengaged little fingers with both of us, turned and left the table, and headed for the bar like a maestro striding onto the stage.

"She's so damn *good*," said Fox admiringly. "To see her in action is a beautiful thing."

I merely nodded my head in agreement. I didn't know what Fox was referring to but I thought she was pretty damn good, too. Seeing her in action, apparently, was about all we were going to be able to do. The noise in the place was such that it was virtually impossible to hear individual conversations taking place at the bar. So I stood at the little table next to a crazy man in flowing blue robes who looked like Jesus on a bad-hair day and I waited for something to happen. It didn't take long.

The first thing we observed was Clyde bellying up to the bar and hailing a busy bartender like you would a taxi on Broadway. Moments later the guy came back, setting a drink in front of Clyde and taking a bill out of her hand on the fly. She sipped her drink and the bartender made his way over to the cash register to make change, acknowledging several other drink orders en route. At this point, Fox left the sanctuary of our table and, like a true urban guerrilla, began creeping stealthily closer to the action. Using various clusters of patrons as cover, he moved nearer and nearer the bar, surreptitiously signaling for me to follow suit.

Feeling like an idiot, I crept through Bennigan's from table to table following Fox Harris as if he were the platoon leader of my new life. At last, we reached a position quite close to the perimeter of the crowded bar, just in time to see the harried bartender putting the change down in front of where Clyde was standing with her drink in her hand talking casually with two guys crammed in next to her. The bartender moved farther down the bar in response to the frenzied demands of the patrons while Clyde leisurely picked up her change and began to count it.

"Now," whispered Fox, hissing intently under his breath. "*Now.*"

Clyde counted the money one more time, then turned and said something inaudible to the guys standing next to her. Then she gazed incredulously down the bar in the direction of the now-vanished bartender, engulfed apparently by patrons on the other side of the bar.

"Do it," Fox hissed. "*Do* it."

Do what, I didn't know, but Fox and I were perilously close to the bar by this time and, following his example, I continued to duck and weave behind other customers so as not to be observed. Fox's appearance being what it was, this, of course, was patently ridiculous. Nevertheless,

Fox persisted in this pattern of behavior and, like a baby chick imprinting upon the path of the mother hen, I trailed along behind him.

"Bartender!" shouted Clyde. "Oh, bartender!"

A new bartender came over to see what she wanted. "How can I help you, ma'am?" he said.

"I think there's been a little mix-up," said Clyde. "I gave the bartender a hundred-dollar bill for a drink and I just got six dollars in change."

"Frank!" shouted the new bartender. "This lady says she gave you a hundred and you gave her six dollars change."

"That's because she gave me a ten!" shouted Frank as he continued pouring drinks.

"Kiss my sweet rebel ass!" shouted Clyde. "I gave you a hundred!"

"That's my girl," said Fox proudly.

The guys at the bar were now clearly rallying to Clyde's side. And who could blame them? Fox and I were inching ever closer so as not to miss a word or a gesture. In fact, just then there was a gesture as Clyde, in seeming disgust and irritation, shot the bird down the bar at the bartender called Frank. This displeased Frank just enough for him to come immediately down the bar to confer with his colleague.

"It's usually not that easy to get a bartender's attention," said Fox.

"Is it possible, miss," said the other bartender, "that you've made a mistake?" Frank himself looked too furious to speak.

"Now close it," Fox muttered next to me. "*Close* it."

"No, it's *not* possible that I've made a mistake," said Clyde indignantly. "In fact, I mark all of my hundreds with my social security number just to keep a personal record. Why don't you check the register?"

By this time a manager type had drifted into the fray and, after briefly conferring with the combatants, walked briskly over to the register and began sorting through the hundreds. After only a moment, he came back down the bar holding a bill in his hand.

"What's your social security number, miss?" he asked.

Clyde told him. He handed her the bill.

"Sorry about the mix-up," he said. "The drink's on the house."

This brought a light smattering of applause from some of the patrons at the bar and Fox and I, of course, joined in. But Frank the bartender was still not happy.

"I don't know how you did it," he said, leaning in to Clyde, "but I know you did it. There's nothing I can do this time. But don't let it happen again."

"Don't worry, Frankie boy," said Clyde in her sweetest voice. "It will."

Back out on the street, Fox and Clyde were both in a mood of high exhilaration and the feeling seemed to sweep through me as well. The lights of the city shined bright with promise.

Anything seemed possible, and at that moment it probably was.

"Not bad for five minutes' work," said Clyde with a beautiful, almost wistful smile on her face.

"It's not the money," said Fox, turning to me as if explaining things to a foreign-exchange student. "It's not even whether you win or lose, Walter. It's how you play the game."

"Yes," I said, a bit uncertainly. "But just what *is* the game exactly?"

"It's a game of dignity and deceit," said Fox. "It's a game of love and death and dreams. I call it the strip poker of life. Got a smoke?"

CHAPTER 5

If you are a writer who currently is not writing, you know what a nightmare of emptiness life can be. If you are fortunate enough to be a writer of the nonfiction variety, all you have to do to get cracking is to focus a bit more narrowly upon your chosen field of study or possibly dig more deeply into your research materials. If fate, however, has cruelly cast you as a writer of fiction, you have myriad madnesses to contend with, for you must cast your net wide enough to capture the stars and you must dig ever deeper into your subject matter, which is, inevitably, the human spirit.

All this being as it may, by this time I was still not writing. Oh, I'd start a page or two, crumple it up, and miss the trash can. But something new was definitely happening in my head. I no longer felt intimidated by the dreaded sight of the blank white page. I no longer blamed my nonlife or the recalcitrant toaster for the fact that I wasn't writing. I wasn't writing simply because I wasn't writing. But that didn't mean I wasn't inspired. And it didn't mean that I wasn't taking notes.

The art of fiction has very much to do with the art

of life as you live it. I recall asking Clyde Potts and Fox Harris more than once why they did the crazy things they did. Clyde would only smile knowingly, stunningly, inscrutably, and with that wink. From Fox at least I was able to extract an answer in so many words, though at those times I believed he had answered only the How and not the Why. I realize now that he responded to both the How and the Why when he said to me: "Everything we do, we do with all our hearts." When you're able to live that way, you'll never experience such a thing as writer's block. I believe I'm getting there, but I'm not there yet.

I wasn't even close to that spiritual destination on that morning four days after Bennigan's when Fox and Clyde came by my place for the first time. It was cold and rainy outside, and when you live in a basement apartment, you can watch just about every raindrop hit the pavement. I suspect that was probably what I was doing that morning when the phone rang and Clyde told me I was about to receive a visit from the two of them.

"We liked your work at Bennigan's the other night," she said.

"I didn't do anything at Bennigan's," I said, suddenly overcome by a sense of misplaced modesty. "You were the one who did all the work."

"Fox and I both agree," continued Clyde, "that you did a beautiful job with phase one. Without the phase-one people, this world would be a pretty uneventful place."

"Well, thanks," I said, taking it as a compliment.

"But that whole Bennigan's thing was small potatoes actually. Fox even said it was just a Zen exercise. This morning we thought we might bring you in on something that could be really fun. A real adventure. Are you up for this, Sunshine?"

I looked around my small apartment. There was an unmade bed. There was a broken toaster. There was a bathroom big enough for a midget without any dreams.

"I'm up for anything," I said.

"You *are* my sunshine," she said. "Be careful what you say to a girl who wants everything. We'll be by in about an hour. So make the bed and put on some coffee."

"That's what I was planning to do," I said. "It's amazing you said that."

"Those aren't exactly unnatural acts, Walter. Besides, I can read you like a book. Speaking of which, when are you going to start the book?"

"Soon."

"Do you know what you're going to write about?"

"No. That's why I always say 'soon.'"

"Don't worry, Walter. I've never written one, but I can tell you this: Writing a book is like falling in love or getting to sleep or finding a taxi in the rain. It'll come to you, but first you have to let it."

After I hung up the phone, I put on some coffee

and made the bed, just like Clyde had suggested. She was probably right, of course. There were no doubt millions of people in the city at that very moment who were putting on coffee and making their beds. Yet it had been strange how Clyde had said what I'd been thinking almost precisely at the moment I was thinking it. It was as if she were standing at the window in the rain sifting through the ashes of my jumbled mind.

And what of Clyde's rather simplistic advice about writing a novel? *It'll come to you, but first you have to let it.* Anybody could have given me that advice. So why did it sound so wise and full of meaning when Clyde said it? Because it came from the heart? Because, as Fox had averred, Clyde was a "veteran soul"? Or was it because I had let myself become a little more attached to Clyde than I'd perhaps realized?

I poured a cup of coffee. Then I lit a cigarette. Then I stood at the window and watched the rain. And what would I write when I started to write? I wondered. Clyde would definitely make a great character. As, of course, would Fox. But how well did I really know these people? Where did Fox and Clyde end and my imagination begin? I stood at the window and watched the rain. In a basement apartment, you can't really see where the rain is coming from. You can only see the raindrops as they splatter on the sidewalk.

Two hours later, I was still watching the rain. Clyde and Fox had not yet arrived. For a punctual person like myself, this was moderately irritating. I had another cup of coffee and another cigarette and I thought about the two of them some more, which was not unusual because I'd been thinking inordinately about the two of them since the two of them had come into my life. The two of them. Were they a couple in the conventional sense? I did not know. I realized it was a stupid question to be asking myself since nothing at all was conventional about them. They seemed to have absolutely no concept of time or money or the law and they bummed cigarettes from me shamelessly. So what was it about them that I found so interesting, even fascinating, and, dare I say it, inspiring? I didn't know. Or perhaps I really did know and I was simply holding out on myself.

A few moments later, the buzzer sounded. I buzzed them in, and a few seconds later, Clyde came in and we embraced with an intensity that I think surprised both of us. Her face and her hair and her clothes were wet with rain, and by the time we let go of each other, so was I. It felt strangely exhilarating, as if her warmth and her wetness were now a part of me, cleansing my spirit, washing away my worldliness. I could see where the raindrops came from before they fell on my sidewalk.

These thoughts were all in a jumble, of course. As practical and as methodical a person as I was back then, I would never have let myself believe that I could be falling in love with Clyde. For his part, Fox wasn't buying it either. He did not bother to even shake hands but went right for the coffeemaker and took the liberty of pouring himself a cup. When he came over to me, his first words were the same as his last words had been the other night.

"Got a smoke?" he asked.

I gave him a cigarette. Then I lit it for him.

"Hate to be a chain bummer," said Clyde cheerfully, "but whatever Fox gets, I want, too."

I gave her a cigarette and I lit it for her. She cupped her hand comfortably around mine as I held the match, and when the cigarette was lit she tapped my hand gently with her finger, as she had done before.

"And whatever Clyde gets," said Fox, "I want, too."

We both looked over at him then, but he was standing with his back to us at the window, just watching the rain.

"Don't pay any attention to Fox," said Clyde. "He just gets moody sometimes. He's basically just like all the rest of us in this stinking world. He only wants what he can't have."

"Right now I want another cigarette," Fox shouted petulantly.

"That's an easy one," said Clyde, casting a doubtful look at Fox, who still hadn't moved from the window. "Hit him again, Walter."

I went over to the window and gave him a cigarette. He took it without looking at me.

"Thanks," he said. "Got a light?"

As I struck a match to light his cigarette, he grabbed my wrist to steady the flame in the same manner Clyde had done, only much tighter, his hand resembling the talon of an eagle clutching its prey.

"The only things you ever really keep in this life," he said, "are the things you let slip through your fingers."

When he let go, there was a small red circle around my wrist, but it soon disappeared.

CHAPTER 6

Sometime later, as we walked through the Village, light rain was falling and it seemed to bring the three of us close together again. Clyde was aiming us toward an Internet cafe that she thought was on a certain street and Fox was ranting that he'd never been in an Internet cafe and didn't want to go in one now because he believed the Internet was "the work of Satan." I was just happy to see us all cheerfully embarking upon a new adventure again. It was almost like old times. Old times, of course, being maybe two weeks ago.

"So what's our next project?" I asked Clyde. "The one you mentioned on the phone."

"'Project'!" Clyde said, laughing rather derisively. "So that's what they're calling it these days."

"I think it's a perfect word for what we do," said Fox, rallying to my defense. "Everybody in this city has a project of some sort or other. In fact, they say when you die in New York, you're not really dead. You're just not currently working on a project. I think it's the quintessential definition of our endeavors on this planet."

"I think you're just trying to suck up to Walter for being an ass earlier, at his apartment," said Clyde.

"Clyde can see into a man's mind like a window," Fox said. "She can bust a guy's chops with the best of them."

"I still think 'project' is the wrong word," Clyde insisted stubbornly. "We're *not* doing what everybody else is doing. They're all just treading water, marking time from cradle to grave without knowing why or having any fun. What we do is more important."

"It's also less important," said Fox.

"Good point," said Clyde. "Sometimes I think what we do is almost an addiction, but really I think it's just our hobby."

"How would you describe today's hobby?" I asked innocently enough.

"Damn you writers," said Clyde. "You're always trying to describe something. Don't you realize that when you capture something in words, you make it disappear?"

"Or someone," said Fox.

"There's not much danger of me describing too much," I said. "I haven't really written anything in years."

"You will," said Clyde. "Soon."

"Windows," said Fox.

The rain had stopped now and the sun was tentatively poking spokes of light between the buildings and walls of the city. Clyde remembered that the Internet cafe was on Bank Street, so that was where we headed. I had a strong urge to take out my little spiral notepad and scribble down a few notes about the previous conversation, but I resisted the impulse. I didn't want to make anything disappear.

"Can I ask a stupid question?" I said.

"There are no stupid questions," said Fox. "There's just a stupid world."

"Okay," I said. "Why are we going to the Internet cafe?"

"That *is* a stupid question," said Clyde, taking my hand and giving it a quick little squeeze. This simple, private, reassuring gesture had a surprisingly visceral effect upon me. It was one of the little wordless things I came to love most about Clyde. It was one of the things, I think I knew even then, that I would miss very much someday.

"We're going there to try to rescue a friend of Fox's," she said. "I'll let Fox tell you about him."

"His name is Teddy M. He's over six feet tall and black as the ace of spades and he looks just like a big, friendly teddy bear. Loves people, loves animals, wouldn't harm a soul. But he's a street preacher, you see. Kind of a wandering park orator who you sometimes see in Washington Square Park or Tompkins Square Park and he's a good one, too.

"I met him some years back. Teddy was in and out of the homeless shelters and we became friends back then because I was in and out of the homeless shelters, too. Of course, that was before I met Clyde, the patron saint of the people of the street."

"And?" said Clyde.

"And so Teddy's got this vision that he lives by, I think he got the idea from the spiritual outlook of Masai warriors or something. It's an African tribal thing, I know. Anyway, Teddy has come to believe that he lives only in the present. To Teddy, there is no past, there is no future. I've come to believe that Teddy may be on to something."

"And I've come to believe," said Clyde, "that Fox may be on to something."

"It's a fucked-up world," said Fox, "and sometimes you gotta just try to unfuck it."

"Where's Teddy now?" I asked.

"Well, that's the problem," said Fox. "He was doing his thing in front of Trump Towers last week and they kept running him off and he kept coming back, so they finally carted him off to the nuthouse, which I know a thing or two about because I used to be there myself. Got out about the time you stopped writing."

I didn't remember giving Fox any time frame for when I'd stopped writing and, though my memory was rather blurry after the tequila binge, I didn't recall telling Clyde either. Maybe I'd told Clyde and she'd told Fox. Maybe he'd been doing some research on his own. Anyway, it wasn't too significant when you compared it to being in the nuthouse so I let it slide.

"He shouldn't have been there in the first place," Clyde was telling me.

"That's what they all say," said Fox.

The Internet cafe was now coming into sight near the end of the block. I wasn't sure how I felt about Fox's revelations that he'd been in a mental hospital and homeless shelters but it didn't really surprise me all that much. It didn't bother me or change anything either. Maybe it was because I believed in Clyde and she believed in Fox. Maybe I, too, believed in Fox. Maybe I was finally beginning to believe in myself.

"Imagine Teddy," said Fox, "locked up in a small padded cell. A guy who only believes—only lives—in the present. He could die in their like the Masai tribesmen used to do when the white man put them in jail. Possibly even worse, Teddy could go crazy. And believe me, I know from experience, when you go crazy, the last place you want to be is in the nuthouse."

CHAPTER 7

Now you might think it'd make you nervous standing right next to a former mental patient, looking over the comely shoulders of the beautiful woman you suspected both of you loved, all of you secretly plotting to spring a current mental patient from a psychiatric ward. But that's not the way I felt that afternoon in the Internet cafe. I didn't really feel nervous at all. What I felt was pure, undecaffeinated excitement, because I was doing something crazy with people who were crazy but didn't give a damn because they knew the rest of the world was at least as crazy as they were. I felt as if I was flying to the stars with Peter Pan or fighting in the jungle alongside Che Guevara and I wasn't dead and I wasn't dreaming and I wasn't alone.

Fox and I were newcomers to the Internet cafe scene, with Fox, of course, still muttering that it was "the work of Satan" and I not entirely disinclined to go along with his thinking. Clyde, however, appeared to feel right at home and she quickly got down to the business at hand. The first step, she said, was to discharge me to the back of the room where a mad-scientist type of character was standing who would sell me three cappuccinos. The place was not crowded and Clyde selected the most isolated workstation she could find. By the time I returned with the cappuccinos, she was already hard on the case.

"I like your idea," Clyde was saying to Fox, "of substituting one of our people for Teddy's shrink at the hospital. It's kind of a variant of the ol' switcheroo."

"Everything in life is a variant of the ol' switcheroo," said Fox. We were now sitting in adjacent chairs on either side of Clyde, sipping our cappuccinos and staring dumbly at the blank screen in front of her.

"Why not let Walter substitute for the shrink?" asked Clyde. "He has a nice practical, rational demeanor and he kind of looks the part. Ever thought about becoming a shrink when you grow up, Walter?"

"What did she mean by that?" I said.

"See," said Clyde. "I told you he'd be good."

But Fox was shaking his head. "I don't like it," he said. "He has no mental-hospital experience, and besides, he doesn't know Teddy. Teddy has a quirk or two that perhaps I neglected to mention."

"Such as?" asked Clyde, hesitating with a floppy disk in her hand.

"Such as he occasionally thinks he's the king of an imaginary African country."

There was a silence in the room. The three of us used the opportunity to sip our cappuccinos somewhat reflectively.

"Jesus Christ," said Clyde. "The shit I do for you."

"For *me?*" said Fox. "It's not for *me!* It's for *Teddy!* I might also add it's for human dignity, justice for all, freedom of spirit, and, lest we forget, good old clean American fun!"

"You're right," said Clyde. "I just lost my place for a moment."

"Happens to the best of us," said Fox. "And you are the best, baby. This is a high-stakes operation, Walter. If you want to bail, now might be the time."

"Walter stays," said Clyde. "If one of us goes down, we all go down. Right, Sunshine?"

"Deal me in," I said, with a cockiness that came from some unexplored territory of the soul.

"Okay," said Clyde. "First we upload the Web page with a photo of Teddy's shrink and a few choice details. What's his name again?"

"Let's see," said Fox, referring to a few crumpled notes of his own. "Here it is. Dr. Stanley Fingerhut."

"Great name," said Clyde. "Now we import a new index. You see, this is the New York State Division of Criminal Justice Web page and I'm simply pretending to have used this account before. I'm going to telnet over to the location where the sex offender Web site is."

"The sex offender Web site?" I asked. "What's that got to do with it?" I glanced over at Fox and he appeared to be equally mystified.

"If Fox is going to take the place of Teddy's shrink, we have to see that Teddy's shrink goes on a little sabbatical. Now since I've telnetted over to the sex offender Web site, it'll think I'm a legitimate state of New York employee and it'll let me make the changes we need to make. Now we put in the floppy disc. Okay, that's one down, one to go. Do you follow me?"

"Of course we follow you," said Fox. "I mean, we may not follow you technologically, but we follow you spiritually. After all, you are our leader."

"I'm not our leader," said Clyde. "In a strange way, I think Walter might be our leader."

"Me?" I exclaimed incredulously. "I'm the new kid on the block. I've never been around people like you and Fox before and I've certainly never before looked at life the way you do or done the crazy and exciting things you two do every day of your lives. I've never even dreamed of doing the stuff you do. I'm the guy who's been busy not writing a book. Remember?"

"We'll see," said Clyde. "There's something you should remember, too. We're not just doing this for Teddy."

The room was silent again. The city seemed to be observing a moment of silence as well. Possibly it was a gesture of respect for the passing of the staid, colorless existence full of quiet desperation that had once been the life of the old Walter Snow.

"Where were we?" asked Clyde.

"One down and one to go," said Fox.

"Right," said Clyde. "Now there's no security on the NAMBLA site. You know what that is?"

"Sure," said Fox. "It's the North American Man/Boy Love Association. They're a sick group of fucks, but I always knew they'd come in handy someday. By the way, here's a good one. Two pedophiles were at a playground one day and they were both looking at a little six-year-old girl on a swing. So one pedophile says to the other: 'She was a stunner in her day.'"

Clyde looked at me and we both laughed. Then she leaned back in her chair, took a deep breath, and ran her fingers through her hair. It was an attractive, natural gesture and it did not fail to go unnoticed by Fox or myself.

"Sorry to be so serious about this stuff," said Clyde. "The Internet always does this to me. It's so easy to superficially change and rearrange things. It's not like life at all."

"I tell you," said Fox demonstrably, "it's the work of Satan!"

"Well, it's good to have someone on our side," said Clyde. "Now we FTP a new index page to their Web site host. And now let's check. Okay. Both locations now list Stanley Fingerhut. That's Megan's Law. Registered sex offenders have to be available to the public. So Dr. Stanley Fingerhut,

Teddy's shrink at Bellevue Hospital, is now, at least temporarily, a registered sex offender. Now we send both sites to the printer. You see, the Internet *can* be fun."

"Wait a minute," said Fox. "I'm starting to feel sorry for Dr. Stanley Fingerhut, though I never thought I'd ever feel sorry for a shrink. Have we destroyed his reputation? What's going to happen to him?"

"Nothing's going to happen to him," said Clyde. "We'll just fax these two pages to the hospital with a little anonymous note—"

"How about this," said Fox. "'Just thought you might want to know that your Stanley Fingerhut has his finger up a little boy's butt.'"

Maybe the Internet was the work of Satan or maybe Fox Harris was Satan himself. All I know is that Clyde and I became suddenly convulsed with raucous laughter and could not seem to stop ourselves even when the mad scientist looked over with a baleful stare. It was just one of the funniest things I've ever heard in my life, and even after all that happened subsequently, I have to confess that it still ranks right up there.

"That's perfect!" said Clyde when she could finally speak. "The hospital will figure this out, of course. But they'll have to lay Fingerhut off for a day or so while they look into it. That's when we make our move. We'll just call in the morning to see if Fingerhut's there, and if he's not coming in, we are."

"Great!" said Fox, with unbridled enthusiasm. "I've always wanted to wear a stethoscope around my neck."

"Shrinks don't usually wear stethoscopes," I pointed out.

"This one does," said Fox.

"You see," said Clyde. "I told you we weren't just doing this for Teddy."

CHAPTER 8

When you're not writing a book, you usually have no idea what it is you're not writing about. Or maybe your mind will fly off in a thousand different directions at once to a million scenes and locations and conversations between contrived characters of invention who have no intention of being remembered by anyone. To attempt such a ridiculous task is to practically guarantee that the result will almost invariably miss the mark, not to mention the wastebasket. In the world of fiction, it is a rare thing indeed for characters to spring up full-blown from the earth and offer their innocence, their nakedness, and their careless suicidal courage to your desperate art. When a novelist who has long suffered the slow death of writer's block is served up these oh-so-human morsels upon a silver tray, it is his blessing and his curse to devour them, lest, no doubt, he himself becomes, inevitably, consumed with eternal regret.

Whenever you introduce live flesh and blood into the secret machinery of fiction, it is bound to become something more than merely a literary procedure. I, of course, did not fully appreciate or understand at the time the nature or the depth of my feelings for Clyde. Nor did I totally comprehend the nature or depth of her feelings for me. I did not know how Fox H. truly felt about me, nor, I must admit, how I truly felt about him. And I still did not have an inkling as to the precise content of the brick and mortar that held so tightly together the relationship between Clyde and Fox.

It is also accurate to say that I had no idea back then exactly where the story was going. All I knew for sure was that I was part of it. And I was proud that I was part of it, and, in a way, I suppose I still am. For I was not merely along for the ride. Though the story flowed wildly like a river over its banks, and I had no control over it really, I was able to capture it. Even in the end, when it lurched terribly out of control, I was able to confine it to those blank white pages, which I would soon observe were no longer intimidating and no longer blank. A typewriter can be sharper than a scalpel sometimes, however. And Clyde, as usual, had not been wrong. When you describe in livid detail a wild, natural thing of human beauty, it does tend to disappear from your life. Maybe every beautiful living moment in your life was meant to disappear anyway. Maybe that's why they last forever.

At any rate, I don't blame myself for what happened. And I certainly don't blame Clyde P. or Fox H. or even Teddy M. I blame the publisher. I blame the editor. I blame the copy editor and the guy who binds the pages together in some factory in New Jersey. I blame the guy who reads the book on a beach in Hawaii. Or the woman who reads it on the plane bound for a trade convention in Indianapolis. Or the guy who sells flowers in the little shop on the corner. Or the guy who buys the flowers for his wife, who's not really on her way to a trade show in Indianapolis but is busy rubbing suntan lotion on the guy reading the book on the beach in Hawaii. Or the people who aren't doing what they ought to be doing, aren't saying what they ought to be saying, aren't living the way they ought to be living, all because they aren't doing what they're doing with any heart at all. If you're going to blame anyone for what happened, you've pretty well got to blame everyone. In fact, you might as well blame the human spirit for flickering each time and looking like it's going to die just before it comes back to life.

I wasn't blind, of course, and I wasn't deaf. I'd taken some notes and these scribblings tend to come alive late at night when you live in a small basement apartment and you find yourself wondering whether to kill yourself or go bowling and, possibly instead, you decide to write. And you observe things, of course, when you find yourself flying perhaps too close to the souls of beautiful, doomed people who embrace you with an open honesty that almost makes you ashamed. The writer of fiction, it would seem, is sometimes like a small child at a formal occasion and he doesn't truly comprehend if it's a wedding or a funeral and in the end, I suppose, it doesn't really matter because the child will soon learn to see and hear and think like everybody else and maybe someday he'll write it all down and make it disappear.

There is another school of thought, of course, probably the prevailing one, which contends that literature and art do not make things disappear but instead make things last forever. Both schools of thought are correct and both are wrong, just as you or I may be correct or wrong and sometimes a little bit of both at the same time. There is no doubt art can cause the idea, likeness, or interpretation of the subject of that art to endure in the minds of men. It is also true, though there is little empirical evidence to prove it, that the very process itself of transmogrifying the muse into the art may mean that the muse has no more further reason for being. These are not thoughts, however, that a writer should be thinking. Not if he wishes to write.

Actually, I wasn't thinking only of metaphysical matters that night. I was thinking of Clyde P. and Fox H. and hammering furiously on my Smith Corona electric typewriter when something happened that gave me quite a turn. I saw a face at the window. When you live in a basement apartment, you realize this may come with the territory but at one o'clock in the morning it can still be a rather frightening event. Someone had not only been watching me write, I had the distinct and highly disturbing feeling that someone, indeed, had been watching me think.

I walked cautiously to the window, acutely aware that I was backlit perfectly for some rambling psycho to blow me away for no rational reason. For no rational reason, I felt a twinge of guilt about the fact that I'd just been engaged in the process of transforming my two new friends into little black etchings in my war against the blank white page. Why did I not view writing about them as a tribute to them? Why did I feel I was somehow using them, changing them forever from people to characters? And what was a character, anyway? It was people, only more so. And I had been doing nothing wrong—only practicing my desperate art, which had been rusting away for many years. Nothing wrong with that, I thought. Everything right. The face was gone, of course. Like all faces in the windows of our lives, it didn't hang around long enough for me to become accustomed to it. And now I wasn't even sure I'd seen it in the first place.

At that time in my life, perhaps understandably enough, I did not have a great many friends. People do not like to hang around with a writer who doesn't write, and the unfortunate soul himself does not much enjoy hanging around people. If he can just avoid hanging himself, he figures he'll be slightly ahead of the game. What I'm saying is that the face in the window, if it had been there at all, and if it didn't belong to the swarthy, crepuscular body of a traveling psycho, must have belonged to either Clyde or Fox and I much preferred that it belonged to Clyde. Yet I did not think that Clyde lived anywhere near the Village. I at first had refrained from pointedly asking where she lived because, I suppose, I did not want to hear that she and Fox were living together. I knew from what she'd told me at the bank that he was her "roommate," but that could mean a lot of things. Maybe she'd met him in his homeless days and literally taken him off the street out of the kindness of her heart, and I believed there was a great deal of kindness in her heart. Now that I knew her better, I still hadn't pursued the nature of their relationship with her because I could never get her away from Fox. Basically, it would have pained me more than I would have liked to have admitted, though it wouldn't have surprised me, to have discovered that they were lovers.

Many thoughts can go through your mind in the brief time it takes to walk out a door and look for a face that isn't there anymore. I found myself hoping that the face had been Clyde's and that she'd now be waiting at my doorstep. This, of course, did not happen. In fact, nothing happened. Well, almost nothing. No one was out there. My author's eye for detail did, however, observe a fat orange cat walking away, toward Seventh Avenue. There was one other thing out of the ordinary. Between the two garbage cans, on the ground directly in front of my window, lay a single red rose.

If the cat hadn't placed it there, then it must have been Clyde, I figured. It is enough to say that I hoped very much that it was Clyde. I took the rose inside and put it on my desk next to my typewriter in a coffee mug filled with water. It smelled of ice cream and perfume and sadness, and I knew that in time, like everything else in this nonfiction world, it, too, would disappear.

CHAPTER 9

The next morning, at ten-thirty as planned, I waited on a street corner adjacent to Bellevue for my two partners in crime to arrive. Clyde surprised me by showing up only twenty minutes late. She was alone and looking beautiful and she put her hands on both sides of my face and kissed me very slowly and very softly on the mouth.

"I love a man who's punctual," she said. "You're the only one in the family who does what he says he'll do when he says he'll do it."

"I would have shown up even earlier if I'd known I was going to get a kiss like that."

"You're sweet, Walter," she said. "You're sweet, and I haven't been perfectly straight with you. Of course, I haven't been perfectly straight with anybody about anything for as long as I can remember."

"Maybe that's part of your charm."

"Maybe. But it's also a burden. Soon, Sunshine. Soon you'll know everything."

"When is soon?" I asked.

"When you finish the book."

"So it *was* you last night. At my window. You left the rose."

"It could've been me," she said. "But for now let's just say it fell off a rose truck and took a lucky roll. But I'm so glad you're one of us, Walter. We need you. I need you. You're practical. You're reliable. You're responsible."

"Yes," I said. "But I'm learning."

Clyde was starting to say something when a vision in blue popped out of the subway and came striding rapidly toward us. Fox, with his flowing robes and hair and a more than usually wild-eyed expression on his face, looked more like a mental patient than he did a shrink. He was carrying, I noticed, a small briefcase.

"Are we green-lighted for wig city?" he asked Clyde.

"I called the hospital early this morning," said Clyde. "Dr. Fingerhut is definitely not coming in today."

"Ain't that the truth," said Fox. "Did you tell Walter that we might need him on the inside?"

"Tell him yourself," said Clyde.

"We might need you on the inside," said Fox. I looked to Clyde but she appeared to be studying a nearby pigeon on the sidewalk.

"What'll I do?" I asked, a bit warily.

"If you can't handle it, just tell me," said Fox.

"He can handle it," said Clyde, taking my hand and giving it a quick little squeeze.

"I can handle it better if I know what it is," I said.

"Simple diversionary tactic," said Fox. "It's easy enough to get *into* a mental hospital. Believe me, I should know. But getting out is a different matter entirely. So once I'm in, I'll need at least some of the security in the place to be focused elsewhere. In other words, we'll need a diversion to siphon some of them to another wing."

"How do I do that?"

"I'd say the more basic the better," said Fox, handing me a small paper bag. "Smoke bomb in the linen hamper will probably do the trick. Give me about a ten-minute lead, though. It'll take me that long to get into my shrink outfit and locate Teddy. Meanwhile, Clyde will be in charge of the getaway car. That'll be a taxi. The plan should be workable as long as Teddy cooperates. By the way, can I bum a smoke?"

I gave Fox a cigarette and this time handed him the lighter. Then Clyde wanted a smoke. Then watching the two of them smoke made me want to smoke. So we smoked on the corner just across the street from the hospital, coolly eyeing the fortress we were about to assault. Standing there with Fox and Clyde, strangely enough, I did not feel nervous at all about the little operation that would soon occur within those walls. Maybe in a certain way, I was already more a part of that small Gypsy band than I realized, because what we were plotting was at least as crazy as what most of the patients inside the hospital were probably thinking and planning at that very moment. At the time, however, I didn't really see it that way. It sounded fairly easy. It even sounded like it might be fun. It did not seem like dangerous or addictive behavior at all. Such was the peculiar nature of the almost magical influence each member of our little trinity appeared to exert upon the others. Maybe it wasn't merely cigarettes we were smoking together on that sidewalk. Perhaps it was the smoke of life.

Before we'd split up at the corner, Fox had given me a bit of a pep talk about how what we were doing was all for the greater good. It was only to lower the odds of springing Teddy, which, he conceded, were not that great. We had to have a diversion and I was the one who'd been chosen to create it. Perhaps he'd seen it as a test of some kind. Maybe I had, too.

Clyde, for her part, was unwaveringly committed to the endeavor. The only advice she'd given me was of a practical nature. If I happened to be questioned by anyone, ask an immediate question of my own in return: "Where's the toilet?" She also suggested that I get out of there quickly after setting off the smoke bomb. I told her I hadn't just fallen off a rose truck.

It was only after we'd separated and I had crossed the street on my own and was standing in front of the building itself that I began to experience a few qualms about joining in on this little hobby. The uneasiness didn't last long, but it was there all right. For one thing, I hadn't even seen a smoke bomb since I was about eleven years old, and the idea of setting one off in a mental hospital, if you stopped to think about it, was just about the height of insanity. It was important, I told myself, not to think about it.

And so I entered the building and headed for the right wing as Fox had directed. Teddy, apparently, was incarcerated somewhere on the fifth floor of the left side of the building. "That's where they keep the monstro-wigs," Fox had said as I departed. "Just kidding," he added. "We're all monstro-wigs." I hadn't found this notion terribly comforting at the time, but thinking about it now, I believe Fox may have been right on the money. Nothing people do will ever again surprise me.

But on that day, as I took a right, then took an elevator, then took the liberty of tossing a smoke bomb into, sure enough, a linen hamper, I was still a novice when it came to being savvy in the ways of the world. I thought that springing Teddy was worth the risk. Later, as I spent more time with Fox and Clyde and even Teddy, I began to believe that almost any prank was worth the risk. It was a dangerous way to live life at times, but it rewarded you with a deeper understanding, whether you wanted one or not.

Feeling somewhat like a demented teenager, I glanced cautiously around a bit to assure that the hallway was empty, then took the paper bag out of my pocket and extracted that most puerile yet effective of all weapons, the smoke bomb. Actually, it was not the most puerile weapon in Fox Harris's little arsenal. He would soon unveil several others that would give the Bellevue smoke bomb a good run for its money. The more juvenile and rudimentary the device, the more proud and pleased Fox appeared to be with its successful deployment. Indeed, in many ways, Fox often seemed to me to be a child living rather precariously in the adult world. I went so far as to mention this to him once and his response was the following: "I wasn't born in a manger for nothing."

The operation seemed to go off without a hitch. I found the linen closet, lit the smoke bomb, lobbed it into the hamper, and headed back down the hallway in the direction from which I had come. I was halfway to the elevator when I ran into a guy in hospital scrubs who looked like a cast member of *E.R.* He stood in the middle of the hallway, effectively cutting off my escape route. I thought of Fox's warning that it was a lot easier to get into one of these places than it was to get out of it.

"Can I help you?" said the man, in that New York tone that makes it clear that helping you is the last thing he wishes to do.

"Where's the toilet?" I asked. An acrid smell was beginning to fill the hallway behind me. I didn't dare turn around to look. But I didn't have to. The guy looked over my shoulder for me.

"Jesus Christ!" he shouted. "The building's on fire!"

I saw the genuine panic in his eyes and I thought about the unimaginable panic that might soon be going through the minds of the mental patients who believed they were trapped in the building. He pushed me aside and ran down the hallway toward what he thought was the fire. I knew we weren't on fire, so I calmly walked to the elevator and took it down to the first floor. Something in the guy's eyes had made me sad, but I didn't dwell on it. There's no time to dwell on anything when you're trying to get out of a mental hospital.

I was about halfway down in the elevator when the fire alarm began sounding in the building. I felt a moment of cold fear as I realized that, fire or not, the alarm system might automatically shut down the elevators, leaving me as a sacrificial lamb once Fox had sprung Teddy. That was one nightmare that, thankfully, did not occur. Unfortunately, another one did.

The elevator doors opened and I walked through the lobby as casually as possible considering I was in a nuthouse that people thought was on fire. I could hear some shouting and screaming by now but I continued my calm exodus of the premises and soon I was outside, where Clyde was halfway down the block leaning against a Checker cab like a cowboy against a fence post. With a stunning smile and a Miss America wave, she motioned me over. It was a best-supporting-actor performance if I ever saw one.

"Don't worry," she said when I got to the cab.

"This is one time when it's a real advantage that the driver doesn't speak English. How'd it go?"

"Pretty smoothly," I said. "Considering."

"Considering what?" said Clyde, crossing her arms and smiling blithely into my eyes.

"Considering that just a few weeks ago I wouldn't have imagined in my wildest dreams that I'd ever be setting off a smoke bomb in a mental hospital."

"Are we feeling a twinge of guilt?"

"Possibly."

"That's not a bad thing," she said softly, cradling my head in her hands. "It's just God's way of letting you know that you still have a conscience."

"What if I don't believe in God?"

"Listen, Walter. There is a God. He's just in a state of deep depression. He has a bad case of narcolepsy. In other words, God is sometimes on the nod. Teddy is a sweet, harmless man who should never have been locked up in this place. What you did was a necessary diversionary tactic that will help him gain his rightful freedom. If God's awake at the moment, Fox and Teddy should be coming out of those doors any minute."

"What if he's on the nod?"

"We're fucked," she said.

She looked around at the taxi driver, who appeared to be sleeping under his turban. Then she glanced again in the direction of the entrance to the building. Then she smiled a sudden crazy smile and her eyes sparkled with some odd brand of cosmic, momentary mischief.

"So you don't believe in God?" she asked. "I doubt if that's true. Maybe you just need a bit of waking up yourself. How about a little vacation Bible class, Sunshine?"

She stepped very close to me then. Our lips and our bodies came together right there on the street in a manner more passionate than I had ever known. I forgot about smoke bombs in mental-hospital wards, taxi drivers in turbans, and everything else in this wretched world as the two of us held each other as closely and as seamlessly as moonlight on a lamppost. As that kiss continued beyond all time, I became quite aroused and began sporting a monstro-erection. This very natural physical reaction, of course, did not go unnoticed.

"You *are* happy to see me!" said Clyde. "Now do you believe in God?"

"I've become an agnostic at the very least," I said.

"Hallelujah!" shouted Clyde. "I've finally found a man who's punctual, practical, *and* he blushes. And he's *still* blushing."

There are times in your life, I suppose, when it's best just to say nothing and savor the moment. Clyde's brown eyes now seemed to fill with galaxies of light, galaxies my dark soul could fly right into and never be found. There was passion, madness, and wisdom in those eyes, qualities distilled from a life lived on the edge of the moment, qualities, I was keenly aware, that were sorely lacking in my drab existence. I needed this woman in a way I could not articulate and, very possibly, did not fully understand myself.

Sirens could now be heard coming up a side street. Moments later, a fire truck had pulled up at the nearby curb. The firemen began running into the building.

"Fox is taking too long," said Clyde. "Something's gone wrong."

Together we ran toward the front of the hospital where, indeed, confusion seemed to reign. Through the glass doors, the lobby area looked like a madhouse within a madhouse. People were scurrying about all over the place and I noticed, as well as the firemen, a police presence beginning to manifest itself. As we gazed up from the front steps of the place, the scene looked like bedlam. There was still no sign, however, of Fox or Teddy.

Clyde took my hand and gave it a quick little squeeze. Her eyes seemed to scan the hospital lobby in vain.

"I'm going in," she said.

"I'm going with you," I heard myself say.

It's always easier to get into a mental hospital than it is to get out of one, and that particular theorem held true on the second time around as well. In a matter of moments, we were standing in the middle of the lobby with mass confusion prevailing all around us. Then two things seemed to happen at once. The fire alarm suddenly stopped sounding and Fox and

Teddy emerged into the lobby from a side door-way.

Teddy was one of the largest, most roly-poly black men I'd ever seen in my life. If I hadn't been looking for him, I never would've picked out Fox Harris. With his hair slicked back, wearing some kind of white butcher's apron, and a stethoscope around his neck, he carried a clipboard and some papers and looked every bit the part of a harried, rather supercilious shrink.

"See how handsome Fox looks when he combs his hair," said Clyde.

"I wouldn't have recognized him," I said.

For his part, Fox pretended not to recognize Clyde and myself. He appeared to be quite absorbed in talking to Teddy and marking down little things on his clipboard chart. He gave a few instructions to an orderly and then began slowly moving Teddy toward the front doors. As he passed us, he stopped for a moment to study his chart.

"I'm going to try to walk him out of here," said Fox quietly, still perusing his clipboard. "If you two will help facilitate Teddy's departure, I'll attempt to stall the powers that be."

It looked for a moment like it might work. Then Teddy, who'd been standing placidly by, on Fox's left side, suddenly sprang to life.

"DEY FOUND ME IN THE CONGO!" he shouted at the top of his lungs. "BEATIN' ON MY BONGO!"

"Relax, Teddy," said Fox. "Just take a few deep breaths."

Fox had placed the stethoscope somewhere along the circumference of Teddy's huge stomach and was listening intently when a hospital administrator walked up. "You can tell a hospital administrator," Fox had confided in me later, "because they always wear a suit and tie and a constipated expression." This one certainly fit the bill. He spoke directly to Fox, ignoring the rest of us.

"What's going on here, Dr.—uh—?"

"Feintush," said Fox brightly. "Dr. Irving Feintush."

"I AM THE KING OF THE ZULU NATION!" shouted Teddy so loudly that even a nearby exiting fireman jumped.

"I'm taking him," said Fox, "for an EKG, an ERG, and a PBP, and, of course, the rather ubiquitous Rorschach test."

"This man shouldn't even be in the lobby," said the administrator.

By this time, things were spinning rapidly out of control. Teddy was chanting a highly realistic-sounding Zulu war chant and Fox was positioning himself between the administrator and the front door. Suddenly, Fox flung away his charts and grabbed the stunned administrator in a powerful bear hug, lifting him off the ground, and thereby at least temporarily deactivating him.

"Run, children, run!" shouted Fox.

And run we did.

Out the front doors and down the steps and down the sidewalk with Teddy in the lead, running with the speed and intensity of a stampeding black rhino, also an endangered species, along the green veldt. In an odd way, it was a beautiful thing to see. A man that large, running with the determination and grace of an arrow aimed at the heart of freedom. I was winded by the time I caught up with him and got him safely in the backseat of the cab. I gave the driver forty bucks.

"Where I take him?" asked the driver.

"Anyplace," I said. "The Statue of Liberty."

As the cab pulled away, I saw a big, peaceful smile on Teddy's face. He stuck his big head out the window and looked back at me.

"Thank you, human being," he said.

I watched the taxi speed away. Then I looked around for Clyde but she was nowhere in sight.

CHAPTER 10

Some women look even more beautiful when they cry. Clyde was one of those. After I'd gotten Teddy safely shoehorned into the backseat of the cab, I hadn't been able to find Clyde anywhere. Against my better judgment, I'd crept back to the now-crowded steps of the hospital and, as casually as possible, tried to peer inside the lobby. The cops were swarming by this time and the focus of their activity appeared to be one Dr. Feintush, who was standing in the center of the lobby apparently trying to bullshit his way out of a situation that had clearly become unbullshittable.

I was well aware that somewhere in that lobby might well be the guy in scrubs who'd seen me in the hallway after I'd planted the smoke bomb. If he spotted me now it would be an easy matter for him to use his powers of deduction and to implicate me as well in the whole mess. But the knowledge that I was at risk was somehow overtaken by my desire to find Clyde and get her safely away from there. It didn't take long for me to spot her forlorn figure leaning against the inside of the glass doors, arms crossed resignedly in front of her, observing the spectacle.

I ran up the steps two at a time and rapped on the glass near her head. She did not respond. She stood like a frozen, tragic statue watching the noose tighten around Fox's neck. Finally, I yanked the door open and she practically fell into my arms. Without a word, like a small child, I escorted her down the steps, where moments later, from a safer vantage point, we watched the cops take Fox away with his hands handcuffed behind his back. He was still wearing the stethoscope, I noticed. It was the kind of detail that a good, observant author would be unlikely to miss.

Now Clyde and I were in a cab together heading downtown in the vague direction of Chinatown and Little Italy. I tried not to stare at her as our taxi hurtled down Broadway, toward Canal Street. Neither of us had yet to speak a word to the other, but that's how it always was with Clyde and me and, to a somewhat lesser degree, with me and Fox. There was an inherent understanding between us that never had to be articulated, that although we were cut from a very different cloth, the very fact of our being together said it all. Some of the most intimate, soul-to-soul communication of my life occurred with Clyde and it always seemed to be at moments when not a word was spoken. That being as it may, I now felt I had to break the silence.

"There was nothing we could do," I said. "I had to get you out of there."

Clyde did not respond. She'd stopped crying but now she seemed to be gazing wistfully out the window at something apparently only she could see. "Windows," Fox had said.

"Where do you want to go?" I asked. "Down to the police station?"

Clyde looked at me quizzically. There were no signs of tears in her eyes.

"No point going to the cop shop now," she said. "Fox has been there before and he knows what to do. He's been taken away in bracelets many times. Been in and out many times. In and out of places. And people."

"Are you one of them?" I asked. Clyde ignored my question.

"We have only one decision to make," she said.

"What's the decision?"

"Where are we going for lunch?"

If the truth be told, I was beginning to feel in pretty good spirits and I knew the reason: the prospect of being alone with Clyde without having Fox Harris anywhere in the vicinity. There was a twinge of nagging guilt, however. Fox was definitely a person of the moment, and not unlike Teddy or the Masai warriors, any amount of incarceration he incurred would, no doubt, be exceedingly difficult for him. I put these thoughts out of my mind, nonetheless, and decided I'd concentrate on Clyde. If she could deal so stoically with Fox's current predicament, so could I.

We got out of the cab on Canal Street, right

where Little Italy meets Chinatown, if the two disparate cultures could ever be said to truly meet. I don't know how cultures or even people ever meet in this busy world. Everyone seems so into his or her self, and the human soul, of course, will remain eternally unknowable. Singles bars are just not going to get it done. Sometimes, though, you meet a rather odd, charming person in, of all places, a bank, and you find yourself walking down Canal Street with her, holding her hand.

"Okay," I said. "Now we come to the decision that all New Yorkers must sooner or later come to grips with. Will it be beef chow fun or linguini with clams?"

"Neither," said Clyde. "I'm a vegetarian."

"Another thing I never knew about you," I said. "How long has this been going on behind my back?"

"Always," she said. "At least as long as I can remember. I've never believed in eating anything that has a face or anything that had a mother."

I looked at her again and it was almost like seeing her for the first time. What a strange and beautiful sentiment, I thought, from such a reckless, fun-loving person.

"Nothing with a face," I said, "and nothing with a mother. Maybe I'll try that myself sometime."

"You will when you're ready," she said. "And I think you're almost ready."

The truth was, I was almost ready to jump her beautiful, sensitive, vegetarian bones right there on the sidewalk. The truth was, I was thinking of becoming a vegetarian myself by having oral sex with a vegetarian named Clyde. I almost said something, but I didn't think it would go down very well, pardon the expression. I was actually quite pleased with that clever little turn of phrase and I took out the small notepad that I'd started to carry around with me. I scribbled some notes to myself rather furiously for a few moments while Clyde wandered off to engage in a conversation with a small Chinese boy carrying a little Italian flag. Maybe the cultures had begun to meet, I thought.

When Clyde came back, she looked almost somber. I put the notebook away and took both her hands in both of mine. Suddenly I was looking into the eyes of a stranger. Just when you think you're getting to know someone, they turn into somebody else.

"Don't write the book," she said.

I was totally floored. Somewhere in the back of my alcoholic memory, a dark thought flashed. I had spent so many years keeping my ideas to myself. Keeping so many pages to myself for so many years. Not speaking my thoughts to others. Not sharing life with others. I couldn't believe she was telling me this.

"I can't believe you're telling me this," I exclaimed. "You're the reason I'm writing the bloody book. You and Fox. Because of you, I have a story. A tale to tell. Characters. Real flesh-and-blood characters. And finally, after all this time, I have a desire to write. A *need* to write. My life was so empty and meaningless, I couldn't even have told this to anyone before. For God's sake, you're my fucking *muse!*"

"That's sweet, Walter," she said. I was starting not to like it so much when she called me Walter. Like Van Gogh, I wanted Sunshine.

"It's not sweet," I said. "It's true. I wouldn't be writing the book if it weren't for you. First you encourage my writing and all of a sudden you tell me not to write. Make up your mind, Clyde. Which is it going to be?"

"Little Italy," she said.

We had a quiet lunch in Little Italy at a place called Luna's. Clyde had some pasta and some minestrone soup. I had linguini with red clam sauce and meatballs, a bad start for my career as a vegetarian. I commented on it and Clyde responded, indirectly, as usual, yet somehow right to the point.

"*If* you go ahead and write the book—"

"I am."

"—then I don't really mind your writing about the fact that I don't eat anything with a face or a mother. I just don't know about the other thing you're thinking of putting in there."

"*What* other thing?"

"The bit you scribbled down while I was talking to the little boy with the flag. It's funny, I guess, in a crude sort of way, and it might even come true if you play your cards right, but don't you think eating a vegetarian is a little bit trite?"

Two things were suddenly in play here and, like any true novelist, I completely missed the second and far more important one, the one that wasn't about me. My work hadn't even been written yet and here it was already being criticized. And not just criticized, but being called the mother of all words that authors hate: "trite." Ho-hum, lackluster, predictable, pedestrian, all those we can deal with. But there's no author alive who doesn't bristle when he hears the word "trite." Any author worth his salt would far rather be accused of plagiarism.

"'Trite'?" I shouted. "*Trite?* What's trite about—"

And then the second, and far more obvious factor dawned upon my marinated brain cells. How could Clyde have known what I'd scribbled in my little notebook? She hadn't seen a word of it. Did she know me so well? Was I that much of an open book? Had she truly read my mind?

Suddenly, I felt a little dizzy and the room seemed a bit warm. What kind of girl was this? I wondered. What kind of person can actually read your mind, tell you what you jotted down to yourself on a little pad thirty minutes ago, and then go on eating her vegetarian minestrone soup as if nothing had happened? And now she was smiling.

"Don't be alarmed," she said. "It was just an educated guess."

"Bullshit. You couldn't have seen what I'd written. What is this? A magic act?"

"I suppose you could say that what you've written didn't go down too well."

I felt as if somebody had hit me with a hammer, but it didn't feel bad; it just felt strange. I retrieved my little novelist's notebook from the inside pocket of my coat. What was the point of keeping my notes to myself? I thought. I might as well wear them on my body like a sandwich board. For a few stunned moments, I carefully perused the words I had recently written.

"It says here 'go down *very* well,'" I said weakly. "Not 'go down *too* well.'"

"Nobody's perfect," she said.

"So just like that you read my mind? I can't believe it. It's got to be some kind of trick. But how in God's name did you learn to do it?"

"Nobody *learns* to do it," said Clyde. "It's just like telling fortunes. It's something I've been doing since I was very young. In fact, I was working in a carnival. That's how I first met Fox. Then the carnival left town."

"Where did this happen?"

Clyde took a cigarette out of my pack on the table. I lit it for her. She took a puff and seemed to just watch the smoke for a moment.

"I think," she said, "it was either in Chinatown or Little Italy."

The waiter came over and we ordered two double espressos, two cannolis, and some of those strawberries you can get in Little Italy that are covered with chocolate. There wasn't much conversation and that was good. I had some serious thinking to do, and since I couldn't know for sure if Clyde knew what I was thinking, I had to be very careful. It was strange, to say the least. But, I must admit, it was not entirely unpleasant. Indeed, there was a rather bizarre sense of excitement about it. It was a new sensation for me. Sharing my innermost thoughts with a friend. Or maybe it wasn't really happening at all. Maybe it was all in my mind.

Suddenly, Clyde clapped her hands together twice, like the CEO of some grand global corporation indicating that the meeting was adjourned. Whatever stray remnants of thoughts I'd had in my mind, I noticed, had also taken their little briefcases and left the conference room.

"Okay, team," she said. "Here's what we're going to do. You're going down to the courthouse and help facilitate Fox's timely release from the calaboose. I really don't want him to stay in there too long this time. It's starting to have a deleterious effect upon his personality. I'd say bailing him out would be the easiest."

"What if I can't afford his bail?"

"Spring him. Like we did Teddy. I trust your judgment, Walter. You have a really well-grounded sense of judgment. You'll know what to do."

"And will you help me?"

"That's impossible. For one thing, I have a rather severe allergy to cops. For another, I've got to get to work wreaking revenge upon the

95

person who got Teddy locked up in the nut-house."

"And whom would that person be?" I asked somewhat cautiously.

"Donald Trump," she said.

There are many weird and arcane strains of logic in this vast and troubled land. But from none of these that made any sense, or so it seemed to me, did Clyde's comments appear to come. Possibly, I thought, I was just too rational, too pragmatic, too *Walter*, to see the light of her peculiar truth.

"Now what in the world," I asked, not unreasonably, "has Donald Trump got to do with this?"

"Trump owns Trump Towers. It was his property and his people who had Teddy arrested and put away in the nuthouse. I'm going to teach Trump that he'd better learn to forgive those who trespass against him. Besides, I never much liked people who always put their names all over buildings. And I don't like the buildings. And there's just a bunch of Gucci crap that nobody can really afford and nobody really needs inside those buildings and it makes everybody who visits here believe that all this capitalistic detritus is what America's all about and they're the only ones who buy it anyway because they want to be how they think we are and it's all Donald Trump's fault."

"Can't argue with that," I said. I wasn't exactly sure what she'd said but it had sounded pretty convincing.

"Don't look so worried, Sunshine," she said

brightly. "I'll take care of Trump and you look after Fox. It's as simple as that. The courthouse is only a few blocks from here, you know."

"But I've never bailed anybody out before."

"Good. It'll be on-the-job training. By the way, I thought you were wonderful today. The diversion worked perfectly. Then you got Teddy on his way safely. Then you even came back and got me. And I'm glad that you did. I'm very, very proud of you, Sunshine. If I still believed in heroes, I swear, you'd be mine."

"I'm nobody's hero," I said. "I'm just trying to figure out what I'm doing and why I'm doing what I'm doing. I mean, these little hobbies of yours and Fox's seem to be becoming increasingly dangerous. The risk involved this morning, as we've already seen, proved to be extremely dangerous."

"Dangerous, yes," said Clyde, taking my hand in hers across the table. "But the most dangerous thing in the world is to run the risk of waking up one morning and realizing suddenly that all this time you've been living without really and truly *living* and by then it's too late. When you wake up to that kind of realization, it's too late for wishes and regrets. It's even too late to dream."

In her eyes, I could easily see her concern for me. It was almost as if she thought that I, not Fox, was the one who was languishing in prison, and maybe I was. She gave my hand a quick squeeze. It worked again. Out of the corner of my eye, I thought I saw her smiling at me in a sad-happy way, like a circus clown smiling at a crippled kid. There was such kindness in that smile. If everybody would have stopped what they were doing for a moment to notice, it probably could have warmed the whole city of New York.

The waiter came and I paid the check and we walked out of the restaurant and drifted down Mulberry Street like two shadows in the cold golden sunlight. I had my arm around Clyde now and I had no illusions that I could control whatever was going to happen. We walked together for a while and looked in windows but I never knew if I was seeing what she was.

I kissed her hair in front of the Church of the Most Precious Blood. Then I kissed her precious hands. My "well-grounded sense of judgment" was telling me that something was wrong with this picture but I ignored it with little conscious effort. It was like a still, small voice speaking to me across my alcoholic dark ages with a message something to the effect of this: that this woman was a ticket for the train to hell. I now realize that no other person can truly be considered a ticket to hell. You choose the path to hell right from the restaurant menu. Then you select the person you wish to travel that path with you.

We walked hand in hand down a block or two, past several funeral homes, onto a small street that ran alongside a park. On one side, young black boys were playing basketball. On the other side, old Italian men were playing boccie ball. I recall vividly the image of Clyde standing in that little park feeding the pretzel I'd bought her to the birds and the squirrels.

"Be careful with us," she'd said. "Fox and I are different from other people. We're like two little birds that you hold in your hand. If you hold us too tightly, you'll destroy us without even knowing it."

I held her close to me then and the birds swirled around us like leaves that were singing. And, I could never be sure, but I thought my heart seemed to be singing, too. The still, small voice was silent now. All the roads I'd traveled in my life, I thought, had led me to this little park and this Gypsy woman who was, I noticed, crying on the shoulder of the highway. And the shoulder of the highway, for the moment at least, was my shoulder.

"Don't cry," I said, kissing her face and tasting her tears. "I'll take care of Fox."

"I'm not crying for Fox, Sunshine," she said. "I'm crying for you."

I left her there in the park and headed down the narrow path to the courthouse. When I turned around to look back, she was gone.

CHAPTER 11

Fox's court-appointed defense attorney looked like Woody Allen. This fact, however, did not apparently surprise Fox. As he confided in me later: "*All* court-appointed defense attorneys look like Woody Allen." Far from holding it against the man, I was just happy to have finally located him. It's troubling enough just trying to bail somebody out of jail without having to witness all the human tragedies occurring in every nook and cranny of 100 Centre Street. I saw a Puerto Rican family huddled together crying. I saw a black family talking to a lawyer. I heard the lawyer tell them: "The best I can get him is five years." Then the black family huddled together and they started crying. Then I saw a small group of Orthodox Jews talking to a lawyer in the corner. The charges, just from what I could tell, had to do with some kind of insurance fraud. The Orthodox Jews were not crying. Maybe they had a better lawyer, I thought.

"Our guy," as the Woody Allen impersonator repeatedly called Fox, was in for criminal trespass, aiding an escape, and resisting arrest. "It could have been worse," said the defense attorney. I looked around me at the scenes of bedlam and despair up and down the long, impassive corridors. I decided the defense attorney may have been right.

"Here's the situation," said the attorney. "The case is before the New York Supreme Court. That's not as bad as it sounds because New York is the only place where the Supreme Court is the lowest court for criminal charges. That really doesn't help things much. It's just a piece of trivia to file away so you'll know exactly where to go if your friend gets himself into trouble again."

"Okay," I said. "But what do we do this time?"

"Well, our guy's already had the first arraignment. The judge has asked for a seventy-two-hour psychiatric evaluation."

"He has?"

"*She* has. Yes. It's not unusual, though. Nothing to be worried about. He'll pass the psychiatric evaluation. Everybody does. You'd have to be Son of Sam having a bad day for New York City to care."

"That's comforting, I guess."

"Yes. Well, there's nothing at all you can do for the next seventy-two hours. I'll call you when it's time to step up to the plate for the second arraignment. The judge will no doubt find no immediate reasons to deny bail. I don't think the bail will be very much. You'll just sign some papers and go home and wait for him and in a little while our guy will be out."

"So I just go home now?"

"That's right. Give me your phone number and I'll call you when we need you."

I gave the defense attorney my phone number and walked down the long corridor past all the troubled and distraught people and went out into the sunlight. It seemed very much like coming out of a sad tunnel of some kind. It was like entering a different land where people laughed and black kids played basketball and old Italian men played boccie ball and if you wanted to go somewhere you could take a cab or a subway or just walk around and look at windows or just look at the sky. Windows reminded me of Clyde and so, for some reason, did taxicabs and the sky and just about everything else. I felt a little guilty that I was so focused on Clyde and not thinking much at all about Fox. But that, I reasoned, was one of the things that happens to you when you're in jail. You find out who your friends really are and, most of the time, the news isn't good.

I went home like the man had suggested. They would call me when they needed me, he'd said. Clyde would call me when she needed to get in touch. She had still not given me her new phone number and I didn't know where she lived, so I had no way to get in contact with her if I wanted to, which I did. Getting in touch with her seemed to be very much a one-way street and the thought rather irked me. My head was also still spinning about Clyde's "educated guess" regarding what I'd been scribbling in my little notebook. If she could truly read minds, she must know how badly I wanted to see her. And, on top of this, she'd pointedly ignored my perhaps crudely phrased question concerning whether she herself had been one of the places and people Fox had been in and out of. This matter regarding Clyde's precise relationship with Fox Harris was beginning to monopolize my conscious thought processes. (This, I realized, was not a particularly healthy mentality for a person to be experiencing on a regular basis.) It was starting to look a lot like jealousy, and jealousy can have a highly corrosive effect upon a human being. Jealousy, however, you must understand, is not necessarily a bad thing for an author.

I began writing like a man possessed. I was starting to connect, I believed, with what I can refer to only as a cosmic creative process. The great writers, the great artists of our time, of all time, I thought, had assuredly been here before. Their unhappiness, their jealousy, their unfulfillment had been the very brick and mortar, the very green fuse by which their great works had been accomplished. Certainly, I did not fool myself into believing that I was a great author or a great artist of any kind. I began to feel, however, a certain emotional kinship with the Great Ones. Of course, I was limited by the God-given talents that God had given me if, indeed, He existed, and if, indeed, He'd given me such gifts. But the circumstances of my own existence were not so dissimilar from Kafka living in his miserable Czech apartment or Poe longing for his long-lost child bride or Van Gogh denied by love; and what of little man Toulouse-Lautrec surrounded by long-legged creatures, to whose world he could never belong; and the sad circumstances of the young girl Anne Frank, scribbling her thoughts in the secret annex of a world turned upside down. And what of Hitler and Gandhi, polar opposites in spirit, both of whom, it could be said, formulated their ideas and did their best work in prison?

There are many prisons in this world, I reflected. One prison was the holding cell Fox Harris currently inhabited; another was the small basement apartment where I now was writing like a man with his hair on fire. No, I did not presume to be a great author writing his great masterpiece. I merely understood that greatness is the result of little people with big spirits who are compensating for what life and destiny have not given them.

So I wrote about Clyde, and to a lesser extent, about Fox, not only as I knew them but as I imagined, possibly even wished, them to be. I experimented with their characters, and what I discovered was that what I didn't know about them seemed to be the very impetus that was driving me on. I needed more pieces of the puzzle, more paint upon my palette to brush onto the canvas. I was experiencing what I took to be the bane of all writers of fiction. Sooner or later, the work must come from within. And that was an area I was not sure of at all.

And so I wrote all that night. Wrote and rewrote. Edited and reedited. I gave Clyde a mouth she didn't have, eyes she didn't have, and, for all I know, dreams she didn't have. I made Fox a mysterious, phantomlike figure, yet a handsome, vital man, consciously keeping my growing personal vitriol out of the equation. And both of them began to materialize before my eyes. They were not themselves, quite, of course. But how many of us can clearly recall numerous times and occasions in our own lives when without any doubt we were not ourselves? It happens all the time. And now, I said to myself, it was merely happening again. Is there anything in our lives so special, so secret, so sacred that cannot be reduced to little black marks like little toy soldiers marching relentlessly like time and war and life itself across the snow-blinded battlefields of blank white pages? How could Clyde say that I shouldn't write the book? It was not only a book about her and her beloved friend Fox, it was a book about every soldier who'd ever fallen on every battlefield and that, my friends, as the years go by, will be every bloody one of us.

Not write the book? I thought. Impossible. The book, it would seem, was writing itself.

CHAPTER 12

No creature in this world is more smug and satisfied than a writer having written. After staying up half the night before, and soundly defeating white page after white page after white page, I felt like celebrating. The only problem was that there was no one to celebrate with. It was true, I'd never really had many friends in the city. This was due in part to my many years of severe alcoholism. It was also due in part to the years I'd spent doing anything (which quite often included doing nothing) to avoid that out-of-control behavioral pattern reprising itself. It was also true, I suppose, that I was never really a very friendly kind of guy. I mean, you probably wouldn't have known it if you'd met me, but down deep it was true. Maybe that's how and why two odd characters like Clyde and Fox could have become so important to me and so close to me in such a short period of time. They were just city workers trying to fill the pothole in my soul. And they almost did.

There were still a few other people I could call, of course, but somehow I just didn't care to.

They wouldn't appreciate what it means when a longtime blocked writer finally breaks through. They wouldn't even understand what it means for a spiritually constipated person to move the neurotic bowels of a lifetime lived in restraint and at last breathe free. Judging, however, from Clyde's recent reticence about my writing the book, I didn't feel that at the moment she'd be the right person with whom I should lift a glass of champagne. She might just christen the whole project by breaking the bottle over the author's head. And Fox, unfortunately, was in no position to celebrate anything.

The book was a very long way from finished, of course. And there were many grammatical errors resulting from my tendency to end sentences with prepositions. Upon rereading a portion of the manuscript, such as it was, I decided to leave all errors as they were and let the prospective editor do his or her job. My job, I reflected, was to not concern myself with plots, or Hollywood, or character development, or pacing, or resolution. What I needed to do, I felt, was to be sure that the book shadowed, or foreshadowed, as closely as mortally possible, the spirit of the truth. I was eager, for instance, to work in a sex scene between myself and Clyde, but I was quite ambivalent as to whether to merely chronicle that steamy scenario when and if it occurred or to write it as I imagined it could be and then wait for life to catch up with art. I did not want the sex scene because it belonged in the movie. I wanted the sex scene, or scenes, because it or they belonged in the book just as the book belonged to Real Life. And Real Life, in a totally unqualified sense, belonged to only two people I'd ever known. And one of them was in the calaboose. And the other one didn't want me to write the book.

As I was drinking my second cup of coffee that morning, the thought of having sex with Clyde Potts came back again to me, recurring unbidden like a vision with a strong visceral component. In other words, I became rather aroused. I hadn't made a conscious effort to think about her. She had, it seemed, come to me. She was unbidden, yet she was certainly welcome. This time I didn't care whether life imitated art or art imitated life. I wanted her in my bed. I wanted her in my book. I wanted her.

I found myself wondering what she would smell like, what she would taste like, and whether a woman with her ultimate street smarts might be equally sophisticated in bed. I found myself wondering if her public hair was as blond as the hair on her pretty head. Or did she dye it, as I'd once read that Marilyn Monroe used to do? I also questioned whether my skills at writing sex scenes might exceed my skills at sex or the other way around. Would the basic sexual chemistry that I felt surely existed between Clyde and myself hold up when tested in the lab? Was there an implicit danger in writing about sex with Clyde strictly from my imagination? Would it color, detract from, enhance, or otherwise alter the act itself if and when it was consummated? Would the book reach its climax before Clyde and I would? Only time and the old typewriter would tell.

The morning drifted on, and after several cups of coffee, I disappeared into the little bathroom to gratify myself. Always before, my imagination had employed a smorgasbord of prurient images drawn from personal experience, porn flicks, wet dreams, and general sordid notions involving many little aspects of many different women, some being fiction, some not-so-fiction. Now the images that inflamed my mind were all of Clyde. It was a feverishly fervent and exciting sensation, almost like being monogamous, as much as that word might apply to your masturbatory fantasies.

I had barely exited the bathroom when the buzzer began buzzing, indicating that I had a visitor. About fifteen seconds later, I saw who the visitor was: the object of my affections. When I saw Clyde, I was glad that I'd just freed the hostages; I might not have been able to contain myself otherwise. To say that I was surprised to see her this soon was an understatement. To say that she looked terrific was also an understatement.

She came into the room oozing so much molecular character that virtually any thinking man had to be captivated. She entered like a field commander, her mind in a more important place, barely acknowledging the room or my presence in it. She was wearing jeans and some kind of plaid lumberjack shirt, carrying a briefcase, wearing no makeup, just an imperious expression that led one to believe she might be high on rocket fuel. Her hair was a mess. She looked like she'd quite possibly slept in her clothes. She looked as tough and sacred as nails on a cross. No one was going to mess with this woman, though anyone who saw her would have liked to have died trying.

"Coffee," she said, placing the briefcase on my desk and then making herself comfortable in the chair behind it. Fortunately, I'd put the manuscript away in a drawer.

"Cream or sugar?" I asked, walking over to the coffeemaker, feeling a bit like a flight attendant.

"Black like my men," she said, without a smile. "Why isn't Fox out of stir yet?"

I stared back at her in disbelief. She held my gaze calmly.

"Because I'm not Matlock," I said as I brought her the coffee. "The judge has ordered him held for the next seventy-two hours for a psychiatric evaluation."

"Well, fuck," said Clyde. "They're finally going to nail him."

"Not according to the defense attorney. He says New York City doesn't care."

"He's right about that," said Clyde as she sipped the coffee. "Got a smoke?"

I lit a cigarette for her and she held my hand, tapping it once gently with her finger. I found this simple gesture oddly comforting, especially in contrast to her rather brusque, oblivious demeanor.

"The attorney says we should have him out in about forty-eight hours," I said. "He'll call me the minute he knows anything."

Clyde inhaled deeply on the cigarette. She leaned back in the chair and ran her fingers absently through her hair and stared at the ceiling in exasperation.

"That bastard," she said.

"Who?" I asked. "The attorney? Fox? *Moi?*"

"Donald Trump," said Clyde.

I poured myself another cup of coffee and pondered that crazy, yet righteous, logic that often emanated from this creature called Clyde and that, just as often, I did not understand.

"So you still have it in for Donald Trump?" I asked.

"Shit yeah, bitch. You bet I do. I have it in for anybody who's crass and un-Christian enough to put their own name on a building or a stadium or a casino. Hell, even a hospital wing isn't too cool. The best gifts always come from that person named Anonymous."

"Couldn't agree with you more," I said. "But that's hardly a reason for a holy war with Donald Trump."

"Don't worry, Sunshine. It's no holy war. It's just a hobby, remember? Sometimes I just get a little overzealous in the pursuit of happiness. That's all. We're just going to have a little fun with the

111

Donald and the best part of it is that he won't even know it. The poor man doesn't realize that he's really a nobody at heart. Remember when he got married and he invited several thousand guests to the most lavish wedding anyone could recall? And the society columnist for one of the papers wrote: 'There wasn't a wet eye in the house.' That was rich, no pun intended."

"All I'm saying is that these little hobbies of yours can sometimes get a bit out of hand. Fox is currently in jail because of the last one. Now you want to go up against one of the richest and most powerful men on the planet—"

"It's more fun that way. Anyway, Walter—if I may call you Walter—I've always believed you should pick your enemies very carefully because who your enemies are tells you more about yourself than who your friends are. What do you think of *that*, Sunshine?"

"I think everything you say or do is divinely inspired."

"I think you might make some lucky girl a fine personal assistant someday. It might even be me if you play your cards right, which you haven't yet, even though I know you're trying."

At this point, she placed one foot on either side of the desk and leaned back in the chair, thus spreading her blue-jeaned legs wide apart directly in front of me. This body language, I thought, was hardly a subtle nuance. She was either signaling that she was available to me sexually or she was teasing me because she knew she would undoubtedly never be available. I tried to remember what it was that she'd been saying. I couldn't for the life of me. And if I stood there gazing down into the canyon of my dreams much longer, no doubt it would be the death of me. For her part, Clyde remained leaning back in the chair, sipping casually from her cup of coffee, holding that quite natural yet highly suggestive position until it made me certain that the whole thing was an erotic dream and I was going crazy and the only way to preserve my mind and body was to go outside immediately and bang my head against the ground until I started laughing or at least stopped looking. If I stayed there, I was in mortal danger of falling to the floor in an old-fashioned swoon. Could it be possible she did not know the effect she was having upon me? Of course she knew. If I'd only known then where all this was heading, I would simply have asked her to take her feet off my desk, which, after an eternity or two, she finally did.

"Let's get crackin'," she said as she opened the briefcase on the desk. "Do you know what this is?"

"I have no idea," I said. "But it looks a bit like it wants to be a garage-door opener when it grows up."

"That's a good one, Walter. Fox may be right. He says you're developing a sense of humor. At any rate, this is the new thing in Europe. It's called a 'phone in a box.' All it is, really, is a cell phone with time on it. You can buy it for a couple hundred bucks. It's virtually untraceable back to the caller."

"Okay," I said warily.

"And this you may recognize as your standard laptop personal computer."

"So we're movin' on up from the Internet cafe," I said. "Where'd you get the laptop?"

"Bar mitzvah present," she said.

With the author's fine ear for detail in dialogue, I felt like correcting her. It was *bat* mitzvah for a girl, *bar* mitzvah for a boy. In Clyde's case, however, she was older than thirteen and she had more testosterone pumping through her than most men, so maybe her little gender bender wasn't such a technical error after all. Nonetheless, I made a note of it in my tiny Jack Kerouac fiction writer's notebook. A fine ear for dialogue is very important.

"Now, traditional methods like Dumpster diving aren't going to work to find what we're looking for. We'll have to contact information brokers. We'll have to pull credit reports."

"And exactly what is it that we're looking for?" I asked.

"Donald Trump's American Express platinum card."

I suppose I knew, even before that time, that these little "hobbies" were someday going to land us all in some very hot water. With Fox still in jail, it now seemed as if the hobbies were Clyde's brainchildren. It was possible, of course, that Fox was running the show even now, like some Mafia don in prison. But all this notwithstanding, the more salient point was why I didn't bail out when I still had the chance. One reason, no doubt, was my fascination, well, maybe mesmerization, with Clyde Potts and Fox Harris. But an even stronger explanation, I now believe, is that if you're a writer of fiction and you go to the well of non-fiction, your wish will come true whether you like it or not.

"I see you're still joined at the hip to your little notebook," she said disapprovingly.

"Yes," I said. "But what did I just scribble down?"

"How the hell should I know? I'm not a clairvoyant. I just have my moments. And in just a few more moments, I'll have the first ten digits of the Donald's credit card. Then all we'll need are the last five."

It didn't take her much more time than she said it would to come up with the first ten digits of Donald Trump's American Express platinum card. She accessed an information broker, pulled up a credit report or two, and, as if by magic, the computer spit out the first ten numbers on the card. I took copious notes in my little Graham Greene travel notebook and every once in a while she shot me a dirty look, but otherwise, the first part of the operation went very smoothly.

"The first ten digits are a lot easier to gain access to than the last five, of course," she allowed.

"Of course," I agreed. Not only did I not know how she was doing this, I wasn't exactly sure why she was doing it. But it was interesting. I got her another cup of coffee and we went through the now-familiar cigarette ritual a few more times. Then she was ready to attack the last five digits.

"The easiest way to get the last five numbers," said Clyde, "is to scam Trump's secretary regarding his monthly charge-backs. These are routine errors, mistakes, and erroneous charges that the credit-card company pays back to the client's account each month. You and I could possibly receive charge-backs, too, but we don't really give a shit. But it's a funny thing about these big shots like Trump. And I've found that it's almost always the case. The richer they are, the cheaper they are. Charge-backs, even if they don't add up to much, are probably the kind of thing he's instructed his people to stay right on top of. That's how I plan to nail him."

"I'm all notebook," I said.

Clyde almost smiled. I took that to be a good sign in general.

"Ten down and five to go," she said, removing the cell phone from its little box.

"Anything I can do?" I asked.

Clyde looked up at me and smiled a crooked, seductive little smile. It was a thoroughly disarming smile, and that always worked with me.

"I'll tell you what you can do," she said. "You can hope I'm successful in scamming this secretary. If that doesn't work, we may have to activate *you*."

I was still conscious at that time that I was being vectored, albeit willingly, ever more wildly into the morass of criminality. But, as they say, knowing something and doing something about it are two different things. I chose to watch, in growing admiration, as this blond pistol of a woman went about her nefarious work. It started out with Clyde punching a number into the cell phone and, while waiting for someone to answer, winking mischievously at me. You might think I would have said something to stop her, but you've got to remember that I couldn't even summon up the courage earlier to tell her to take her feet off the desk. So I just smiled back. It was a safe thing to do. It probably wouldn't have made any difference anyway. Some things are written in books and some things are written in the saltshaker stars and there's not a damn thing you can do about either one of them once they get past the editor.

"Hi," Clyde was now saying. "This is Mindy from American Express platinum customer service. We have a notation here of a number of charge-backs to your account for last month, but because of a computer crash the records have been lost. You're one of our priority customers, of course, and we just wanted to give you the opportunity to resubmit them."

Clyde gestured to me for another cigarette. As I gave her a light, it occurred to me, not for the first time, that she was a pretty cool customer herself, possibly the coolest I'd ever met in my life.

"Yes," she continued. "I thought that you might. It's no problem at all. We just have to verify your identity. For security we'll need the last five digits of your card-member account number and the expiration date."

A short time later, Clyde terminated the call with a look of pure triumph on her face. Maybe "pure" is not quite the right word to use in this description. To my naked author's eye, there was an almost blinding sexual energy in her countenance as well. As a man, I knew that I wanted her more than I ever had before.

"You got it all?" I asked.

She put her two thumbs together at the tips, raising an index finger on each hand like a small goalpost that she held at arm's length in front of her.

"Touchdown!" she said.

"What do we do now?" I asked.

"Now," she said, "we're going to have a party."

CHAPTER 13

The Unicorn was a seedy-looking little Irish pub about two blocks from my apartment. I'd walked past it many times without ever having had the inclination to go in the place. Now, with Clyde by my side, and fully off the wagon, I was totally prepared to walk past it one more time. But Clyde, apparently, had other ideas.

"What a cute little place," she said. "What's it like inside?"

"Don't know," I said. "I've never been in there."

"Only you, Walter Snow, could live a block and a half away from a place called the Unicorn and never bother to go inside."

"You forget, darling, that I haven't been drinking for almost seven years. That is, until I met you and Fox Harris."

"That's right. Blame somebody else. Every alcoholic in the world does that. Can't you come up with an original excuse? For God's sake, Walter, you're a writer!"

"I haven't come up with anything new or original to write in seven years either."

"Until you met me and Fox Harris. Are we your curse or your salvation?"

"Read the book and find out," I said.

But Clyde was already marching, like the general of an invading army, into the little bar. I almost felt like a husband then. A husband who'd had a little misunderstanding with his wife maybe. It was something I had never felt before. I hesitated for a moment on the sidewalk, watching this person I hadn't known all that long and whom I didn't know all that well walk away from me, knowing I would follow. And what if I didn't? If I just kept walking down the street? If I actually took the chance of letting her disappear from my life?

You could say that I thought of that moment as a chance to get away, to break the bonds of our fateful trinity that even then, I knew, like that biblical garden, contained the seeds of its own doom. Unlike Fox and Clyde, I tended to believe what was written on the seed packet, but I did not truly want to get away from them because there was nowhere else I wanted to go and no one else I wanted to be. It was a beautiful friendship the three of us had, actually. None of us dreamed anyone would really get hurt. "Dreams will never hurt you," Fox once told me. "Only the dreamers can."

But for reasons that perhaps I did not clearly understand, there was never any doubt about how I felt about Clyde. At that moment, I reckoned that I could no more walk away from Clyde than walk away from myself. And I couldn't walk away from Fox either, for that matter. It was as if the three of us somehow were children who had taken a blood oath to stand up for each other, always. That kind of love or loyalty has no sell-by date, has no rationale, has only what is written in blood, written in the wishing stars of a destiny that time and the world could not sustain.

"What took you so long, Sunshine?" said Clyde, not waiting for me to answer. "This place is perfect!"

I glanced around to see what Clyde was so excited about. It was one of the dingiest bars I'd ever seen. It was a mom-and-pop place without the mom. But the pop was there all right. He looked like an ancient leprechaun standing behind the old battle-scarred bar and, a mildly disturbing vision, even to an ex-drunk, he appeared to be far more inebriated than the three other persons in the place.

"It's seldom a good sign," I said, "when the bartender's drunker than the patrons."

"Maybe Jesus is telling us to catch up with him," said Clyde.

"This doesn't look like the kind of place Jesus would be caught getting resurrected in."

"I didn't think you believed in God."

"I may not believe in God, but I believe in you."

"That'll work," she said. "Just so you believe in something."

We sat at the bar and ordered two pints of

Guinness. It wasn't long before Clyde was chatting up the colorful fellow behind the bar. It wasn't long after that before she had him completely under her thumb.

"I've been on the piss for about a week," he allowed. "Some blokes in suits and ties have been coming around—"

"That's always bad," Clyde put in as the leprechaun set the two Guinnesses down on the bar.

"You're not shittin', lassie," he said. "The bloody bastards are trying to close the Unicorn. I'll never let 'em close the Unicorn. Had this place for thirty-two years. If they close her, they'll have to bury me with her. Then I would never get the opportunity to serve another Guinness to such a beautiful lass with eyes like an Irish morning."

"Who are these people who're trying to close you down?" asked Clyde.

"Wankers," said the leprechaun. "Bloody wankers is what they are."

"I know what they are," said Clyde. "What I want to know is *who* they are."

"Lawyers for some big corporation," he said. "Very dodgy blokes. Causing trouble with the health inspector, the fire inspector, the bleedin' landlord. I don't know who they are, is the truth. They're wankers and they won't tell me who they are. That's why I've been on the piss for a week."

"Sunshine," said Clyde, staring at me with eyes that, indeed, appeared to resemble the beauty of an

Irish morning. "I think we need to look into this matter."

"Don't we have enough hobbies going at the moment?" I asked.

"Don't be cynical, darling," she said. "It doesn't suit you."

It was the first time Clyde had called me "darling" and I grasped hold of the word like a drowning man, which, looking back on things now, was not such a bad analogy. (Or was it merely a simile? This is the kind of thing that an author really should know but almost never does. Most of the time it is best left as a question mark for the editor to resolve. This makes the editor feel important and needed and, in fact, is the brick and mortar that justifies his or her existence. Unfortunately, it is never quite that easy for an author to justify his or her existence. That's why they are often such unpleasant or merely unremarkable people. That's also why, if you like the book, you should never meet the author.)

I was oblivious to it at the time, but there was a fine Italian hand pulling the strings and adjusting the mirrors behind the little hobbies of these two new friends of mine who had done their best to fill the emptiness of my own fairly unremarkable life. Again, there is no useful purpose in assessing the blame for what happened. Certainly, we all must shoulder some of the blame for the choices we make and the company we keep. Yet how was I to know that helpful, wholesome concepts, such as friends and hobbies, could lead one down the path to Satan? Of course, if you don't believe in God, it's highly likely that you don't believe in Satan either and, I suppose, I didn't. Today, I'm not so sure.

By the second round of Guinnesses, Clyde was buying drinks for the house, which wasn't really so difficult since there were only three other patrons in the place. By the third round, I felt like I'd known the owner and proprietor, one Jonjo Mayo, all my life. By the fourth round of Guinnesses, I'd lost track of what round it was. That was possibly the main reason I let myself get involved in Clyde's newest little hobby, to save the Unicorn.

"I don't think I'm overloading your plate," said Clyde as we stood by the jukebox listening to music by the Irish Rovers. "You've already promised to help Fox but there's nothing anybody can do until you hear from the attorney. So, in the meantime, all I'm asking you to do is a little investigative work to find out who's putting the squeeze on our friend Jonjo. I mean, you practically live next door to this place. It'd make a perfect club-house for us once Fox gets out. Will you look into it for me, Sunshine? Please?"

"Is this how I play my cards right?" I asked.

"No," she said, looking absolutely heavenly in the celestial light of the jukebox. "This is."

Then she kissed me like I'd never been kissed in my life. Her tongue slipped between my lips like a silken butterfly and I felt like I had woken from a lifetime of slumber and into the midst of a fragrant

Irish morning even though I noticed that her eyes were closed. I closed my eyes, too, and the silken butterfly seemed to be flitting around inside my head, like pink wings touching places and things and dreams that I'd forgotten I'd forgotten.

"That was a hell of a party," I said, sometime later as the two of us stumbled out the door of the Unicorn.

"That wasn't the party," said Clyde, laughing a carefree laugh that sounded to my Guinness-enhanced consciousness like a beautiful crystal bell inside my head. "That was just the mixer. I've already decided we'll have the party on a much more lavish scale. Trump will pick up the tab, of course. There'll be thousands of guests. All the homeless people at the Old Armory where Fox first met Teddy. In fact, Teddy can be the guest of honor."

"If we can find him," I said, a trifle doubtfully.

"Oh, we can find him," she said. "We can do anything!"

Once again, I had to admire this woman, so confident, so charmingly childlike, so appealing to me in her veil of crazy courage. Maybe we *could* do anything, I thought. My creativity, my happiness quotient, my hope for the future all seemed to be redlining because of her. The only thing that nagged at me slightly was the knowledge that, as a former AA person, drunk out of my mind on Guinness, I was clearly backsliding in the sobriety department. But I felt so happy.

"Jesus," I said. "If only my sponsor could see me now."

She smiled that wistful, rueful, stunning smile that could beat the world. She looked me straight in the eyes.

"Don't worry, Sunshine," said Clyde. "She can."

CHAPTER 14

You'd think it might be difficult for a newly converted vegetarian living in a basement apartment to cough up ten thousand dollars for the bail of somebody he hadn't even known a month before. According to Fox, however, he and I had known each other for thousands of years. Of course, he wasn't the one who had to cough up the ten thousand dollars. But let's take one thing at a time.

I will admit that I became a vegetarian during roughly this time frame because of Clyde's influence. All of us are influenced by the people around us and the people who are closest to us, and I, like anyone else, am no exception. It was more than just Clyde's earlier comments about not eating anything with a face or a mother, however, that caused me to make this change in my eating habits. "Not eating animal pain," was one way she had described the reasons for being a vegetarian. But, in truth, that wasn't the thing, laudable as it may be, that swung me. The thing Clyde suggested, and the aspect of being a vegetarian that I clearly liked the best, was the undeniable moral superiority you feel toward all the other poor devils who are not vegetarians like yourself.

In time, I came to feel morally superior to a great many people, including, I freely admit, Clyde and Fox. This had little to do with vegetarianism but a great deal to do with what happens when modern boys and girls learn the rules of the road. Today, it's hard for me to believe that I could have been irritated when I first learned that Fox was also a vegetarian. I once considered this to have been merely jealousy on my part. Now I think it had something to do with every human being's inexorable drive, whether conscious or unconscious, toward moral superiority. Remember, Hitler was a vegetarian, too.

On the morning following our Guinness marathon at the Unicorn, I got the call from Fox's court-appointed attorney. I won't bother you with every little trivial detail, but instead, I'll just try to give you an overview, or should I say underview, of this rather tedious experience. The first thing I did was take a cab to 100 Centre Street, where, after wandering in the labyrinth for a good while, I was able to locate Woody Allen lurking outside a small courtroom. He told me that since Fox lived in New York and was not a violent offender, he thought he could very conceivably get him out without bail. I thought that was good news. Unfortunately, both of us were wrong.

Woody Allen also told me that if a small bail proved to be necessary, I would legally "own" Fox

Harris. As long as he didn't flee the jurisdiction and fail to show up in court, any money I laid out for bail would be returned. The attorney nattered on for a good while about what might or might not happen to Fox Harris and myself and other hypothetical defendants and their good angels like myself. It was all fairly boring but I did my best to give the semblance of listening intently. Finally, we entered the courtroom and the proceedings began.

The proceedings proceeded ploddingly along until at last Fox was brought out and Woody Allen went forth and did his thing and the judge said he found "no immediate psychiatric reasons to deny bail." Fox, having already pleaded "not guilty," was thereby ordered released on one hundred thousand dollars bail. I did some quick calculations in my brain and realized that I was going to have to come up with ten thousand bucks. It was just a good thing, I thought, that I didn't have any kids and they didn't have any college tuition. Fox gave me the double thumbs-up, which is not such an easy gesture from the somewhat compromising position of wearing handcuffs. I did my best to smile back. Privately, I realized that ten thousand dollars represented most of the money I had in the world. If Fox Harris decided not to show up in court, I would own him and that would be about it.

The judge banged her gavel for about the fiftieth time that morning and they took Fox away and I waited some more for Woody Allen to file another motion or gather his papers or whatever you do if you're a court-appointed defense attorney who vaguely resembles Woody Allen. I felt a bit sorry for the guy, if the truth be told. I also felt a good bit sorry for myself. I did not, I should say for the record, feel sorry for Fox Harris.

Eventually, Woody Allen emerged from the courtroom and directed me to a small office down the corridor where I would supposedly be separated from my ten grand. I'd had a little time to think about it and I now didn't require Woody to tell me that paying bail for anybody was a fairly dicey thing. Maybe I "owned" Fox Harris, but, in a sense, he also owned me. On any crazy whim of his, I'd clearly be out the whole ten thousand. I knew how impetuous and unpredictable Fox was as a human being, and it did not give me great comfort. Those qualities helped to make him a colorful, spontaneous character, but they also made him a bad risk for bail.

I waited in a long line. I asked myself why I was doing what I was doing. I knew it had to be either a humanitarian gesture or simply for Clyde. I decided I *was* doing it for Clyde, always with the stipulation, of course, that I was doing a lot of things these days that I never thought I'd be doing and I didn't know why. One of those things was writing a book, and it mildly grieved me that I could have been home writing if I hadn't been forced to stand here waiting in line to be fleeced of ten thousand dollars. But nobody was forcing me, I reflected. And if I hadn't been involved with Fox and Clyde, I wouldn't be writing the book. I decided it made its own peculiar sense for me to be waiting in this line. As Fox would later tell me: "Everything comes out in the wash if you use enough Tide."

At last I got to talk to the court officer and I gave him Fox's case number and I started to pay with a check but he wouldn't take a personal check so I had to max out my credit card. Then I had to sign some papers. Then he told me that Fox would be released shortly and that I could go home, which I did. But I didn't go directly home. I stopped, oddly enough, at the Unicorn.

I figured there was time for a little of the hair of the dog that bit me before a fox got out of jail and bit me again. The Unicorn was empty, as usual. This time, only Jonjo was there, polishing a few glasses rather wistfully. I ordered a Guinness and thought I'd listen to his sob story for a while. It was the least I could do for Clyde, I found myself thinking. Was I just a chemical puppet doing everything for Clyde? I tried not to think too hard about it. I tried just to concentrate on drinking my Guinness and listening to Jonjo's sorry tale.

"Been on the piss since you last came in with that lovely lass," he said. "Where the hell is she, by the way?"

"Probably having brunch with Donald Trump," I answered, gulping the Guinness.

"It's gonna take Donald Trump to keep me little Unicorn alive," he said ruefully. "Those wankers came back again."

"Who are those wankers, Jonjo? They're not from the mob, are they?"

"Sweet Leapin' Jesus," said the leprechaun. "If they were from the mob, I'd've paid 'em off already and been done with it. The mob at least gives a bloke a chance. These wankers won't stop until they kill the Unicorn."

"You mean they're not after a payoff?"

"Hell, no. They're out for me blood. They won't be happy until me and me dear little Unicorn fly back to Limerick together. They won't take money. What they're after is me lease. The health department came by again yesterday after you left. Now the zoning authority is paying a visit this afternoon. No, me lad. These wankers are not from the mob. These wankers are from corporate America!"

I ordered another pint of Guinness and reflected darkly upon the nature of the people who would threaten a modest little establishment called the Unicorn. A few regulars began to drift in but it appeared as if all the harassment was starting to atrophy what precious little clientele the Unicorn had to begin with. In a way, I admired Clyde's strange brand of courage and humanity in standing up for the underdog. In examining the complex nature of her character, I recalled a comment she'd made during our maiden visit to the Unicorn. I'd mentioned in passing that I thought the place looked like a hopeless cause. Her response, delivered quite archly, had been: "Hopeless causes are the only ones worth fighting for." Her judgment might be somewhat askew, but you had to admire her spirit.

"Here's the card one of the blokes left," Jonjo was saying, pushing the business card across the bar. "He said if I decide to sell him me lease, to just give him a call. I'd just as soon sell him me bloody lease on life!"

I looked at the card. It read: "Stanton Malowitz, Northwest Properties, Limited." There was a phone number with an area code I didn't recognize. I wasn't much on detective work, but if I was going to run down any leads for Clyde regarding the fate of the Unicorn, this looked like a good place to start.

"Keep it, me lad," said the leprechaun. "I'll not be calling him."

I had one more Guinness, told Jonjo I would return, and toddled off toward my apartment. I'd forked over ten grand for Fox's bail and done some snooping at the Unicorn, and the nagging feeling that I might be being used by Clyde had vanished in the light of my good works and, very possibly, the Guinness. Would I have done these things for anyone else? Probably not. Without Clyde's encouragement, I doubt if I would even have done them for myself.

CHAPTER 15

From far down the street, I could see already that Fox Harris was lounging on the front stoop of my building. He was smoking a cigarette and he didn't look like he had a care in the world. Certainly he didn't appear to be a man who'd just completed a seventy-two-hour enforced accommodation in a holding cell. He looked like the king of the Village. As I got closer, he motioned grandly for me to take a seat beside him on the stoop. I did.

"Try one of mine," he said, opening a heart-shaped silver locket and grinding the tip of the cigarette into its unseen contents. "It's a new Australian aboriginal brand called Malabimbi Madness."

He held the cigarette-shaped object in his hand for a moment, turning it over and over. He seemed to be mulling over carefully what he was going to say next. I waited patiently until he finally spoke.

"I guess I should thank you, Walter," he said, "for bailing me out. So I will thank you. Thank you kindly. It was you who bailed me out, wasn't it?"

"Clyde's idea," I said. "My money."

"I'd like to say it'll come back to you tenfold, but I'm not sure it will."

"It's not a problem," I said. "Just don't flee the jurisdiction." Fox laughed.

"Flee the jurisdiction?" he said scornfully. "No one in the history of mankind has ever been able to really do that, I'm afraid."

"Just see that you're not the first."

"Yes, sir," he said, throwing me a jaunty left-handed salute. "Now let's see if you're ready for some Malabimbi Madness."

He handed the object to me. We were sitting only a few feet away from people walking by on the sidewalk and it made me a little nervous but I wasn't going to let him know.

"Okay," I said. "What is it? Where'd you get it? And what do I do with it?"

"Aren't you the question man," he said. "It's called a one-hitter. I got it from friends in the sneezer as a going-away present. And what you do with it is you smoke it. Just pretend it's a regular cigarette. You can do that, can't you?"

I ignored Fox's condescending tone. I had no idea what he'd been through in the "sneezer," as he called it, as I had no idea what Fox or Clyde had been through during the courses of their lives. They were like waves in a misty sea and I could never seem to quite get beneath the surface of their being. The sea analogy was a good one, I thought, with some little measure of authorial pride. For they were anything but shallow people. And it was their very depth as human beings, I reflected, that made it difficult to discover who they truly were. They were almost easier to write about than to actually know. I did not take out my notebook but I made a few mental notes about Fox's apparent hardening of attitude toward me.

I turned my full attention to the object in my hand, the "one-hitter," which Fox proceeded to describe. He also claimed that just a few puffs on the device would make you so high "you'd need to contact somebody from *Star Trek* to help you find your head."

There has always been a paradox inside my soul. I'm basically a cautious, rather conservative person. On the other hand, there are times when I'm willing to try anything. For whatever the reason, this appeared to be one of those times. I took one deep hit off the one-hitter. It was a pretty amazing device, all right. It looked just like a cigarette, down to the smallest detail, but in reality was a hollow metal tube painted white for the cigarette and brown for the filter and as soon as I took the first puff, all my paranoia and misgivings about smoking dope on the stoop of the building, about Fox Harris, about the world in general seemed to disappear with the smoke of the Malabimbi Madness. I was never sure from that point on whether the euphoria I experienced was on account of the Malabimbi Madness or the idea of the one-hitter itself. All I know is that I was to use the device many a time with Fox and

Clyde in the daunting days to come and it often seemed to free me, if only for a while, from the sad and stifling bonds of this tedious and sometimes terrible world.

"See the people on the sidewalk?" Fox asked. "Now take another hit and keep lookin' at 'em. What do you see?"

I took another hit and kept looking at the people. The one-hitter was having a powerful effect on me but the people still looked like people. Just normal people, going to lunch, coming back from lunch, going to work, going wherever normal people go in New York. I was suddenly glad I wasn't one of them.

"Aren't you glad you're not one of them?" asked Fox.

I was too stoned not to be stunned or maybe I was too stunned not to be stoned. Either way, it felt like somebody had hit me on the head with a croquet mallet. Was it possible that I was so shallow of emotion, so transparent in countenance that both Clyde *and* Fox could seemingly read my mind? It was *not* possible, I figured. The guy had merely made a lucky guess. But wasn't that what Clyde had said? That she'd merely made an educated guess? This was really more than I could deal with before my vegetarian lunch.

"They're all so self-importantly going nowhere," Fox was saying as he retrieved the one-hitter from my grasp, took another hit, and studied the passersby. "They just have no idea of who they are or where they really belong. Nothing will ever be enough for them. Nothing will truly make them happy. They all think they've got to get someplace, got to meet someone, got to get to work, got to get home, got to keep that appointment. If they had a hundred million bucks, it wouldn't be enough for them. If they had four cars, they'd need more. If they had four homes, they'd need more. They are organically out of touch with their land and their tribe."

Fox passed the one-hitter back to me. I took another deep hit and listened as his diatribe continued. The more hits I took, the more sense he seemed to be making.

"It's like Gandhi said about the West. He always called the West 'the one-eyed giant.' The West had all the great, important, modern things going for it, like science and technology and money. All the East had going for it was a kind of basic primitive wisdom that had grown up over the centuries, interlocking the land and the people in ways the West could hardly imagine. The people of the East were grounded in that wisdom, while the West was built on a shiny edifice of science. So it's very possible that the people in the East might not understand what really causes an eclipse of the sun. They might attribute it to an act of God or gods or fate, and panic might ensue, almost like the kind of panic engendered by a stock-market crash over here.

"But what's important, Walter, is that the people

of the East generally feel an organic belonging to the land and the family and the tribe. They know who they are and have a good sense of where they belong and how they relate to life and land and love. Only the one-eyed giant thinks that one man needs to own two hundred radio stations or a whole string of shitty chain stores or restaurants. Only the one-eyed giant has five houses and never feels at home. These people walking by don't have a clue as to what they want. The only thing you can bet on is that if they ever discover what they want, they're going to want more and more and more, out of all proportion to their true organic need.

"I've known about the one-eyed giant for a long time. So has Clyde. The Indians who lived here before us, right here in Manhattan, knew themselves and their place in their world far better than we do today. So Clyde and I try to think the way they would if they were here now. We try to live our lives according to what we believe are our true organic needs. Am I boring you?"

"Not at all," I said honestly. It was a side of Fox Harris I'd never really seen. If his occupation was that of troublemaker, here was the motivation behind his rather odd career.

"You know what I'd like to see you do?" asked Fox.

"Give you back the one-hitter?"

"No. I'd like to see you meet your own personal organic need. I'd like to see you write another book."

139

"That's great," I said facetiously. "Clyde tells me *not* to write the book. Now you tell me to write it. Maybe you two should get your signals together."

"Believe me," said Fox, "our signals are together. But Clyde is a very intuitive person. She's also an extremely quick study. She's also a very beautiful and intelligent woman. But she isn't who you think she is."

I thought for a moment about Fox's rather cryptic remark. I, to be totally truthful, had no idea who Clyde really was. I only knew that she was becoming alarmingly influential in my life. Not that I wanted or could have caused her apparent powers over me to cease. Whoever she was, I reflected, I needed her in my world.

"Okay," I said at last. "So who is she? All I know is what she told me. She was telling fortunes in a carnival. You met her at the carnival. Then the carnival left town and the two of you stayed."

Fox looked at me quizzically, almost as if he were sizing me up spiritually. It was not a particularly comfortable feeling. It appeared as if he were trying to decide whether or not to respond. Finally, he did.

"Carnival?" he said rather whimsically. "I guess you could call it that if you wanted to. But it wasn't really a carnival, you see. It was a drug rehabilitation center, Walter, for hard-core heroin addicts. It was outside Tucson, Arizona. I was working there as a counselor."

For some reason, I didn't want to hear Fox tell

me anything more about Clyde. But part of me, in a total spirit of ambivalence, wanted to know everything about her. And Fox knew her better than anyone. Indeed, as she'd once told me, Fox knew her better than she knew herself.

"And Clyde?" I asked. "What was she doing there?"

"I think you know the answer to that, Walter."

He had said it not unkindly. As I looked at him then, he met my gaze. Then he nodded, a little sadly.

"You mean," I said, "that Clyde was a heroin addict?"

Fox put his thumbs together in front of his face. He raised his two index fingers straight up like little goalposts.

"Touchdown!" he said.

CHAPTER 16

Her panties were black and shiny and wet and tasted like salt and sugar and cinnamon and some indefinable spice that was far more exotic in its effect upon my senses. I had, quite literally, chewed her panties off, knowing full well that they would only be an appetizer. Her bush was dark and verdant. It was obvious that she did not peroxide her pubic hair in the fashion of Marilyn Monroe. I licked it deliriously, desperately, like a man in a desert lapping up a mirage. I could feel the animal heat emanating from her thighs and burning my face like a furnace. I paused for a mere moment to glance up at her face. Clyde's eyes were flashing like a tiger's. I went back to my delicious work, not daring to gaze up again.

I thrust my tongue deep and I thrust my tongue shallow and I lapped her up from stem to stern. She took my head in her hands and held it tightly against her snatch and I toiled away like a prisoner of ecstasy until at last the little man in the boat seemed precariously close to being thrown overboard. I tried to move up on her and mount her but she held me there with the strength of a mad Amazon. Her back arched suddenly and she screamed with a strange, muted, almost feral growling sound and her fingernails embedded themselves deeply into the sides and back of my neck and still she held me there against the molten mouth of a vaginal volcano. Find there was nowhere else I'd have rather been. It's a dirty job, I thought to myself. It's a dirty job and I get to do it.

I ripped the page out of the typewriter but I did not throw it away. Sipping a tepid cup of coffee, I read the pages by the light of the floor lamp, pacing nervously back and forth in front of the darkened window. It was almost an embarrassment to read what I'd written. It read like a bad attempt at a steamy sex novel. And yet I'd written it and I felt oddly hesitant about getting rid of these passages.

What if I was crumpling up Henry Miller? I thought. What if I was about to toss D. H. Lawrence into the trash? Who was I, the mere author, to decide what was good or bad or great writing? Let the editor cut it out. Or better yet, fuck the editor. Let the critics decide. And if the critics don't like it, fuck the critics. No kid in the world ever grew up wanting to be a critic anyway. And there's never been a statue erected to a critic.

There's probably never even been a penis erected to a critic.

I lit a cigarette and heated up the coffee. It was two-thirty in the morning and here I was pacing my tiny apartment like a man in prison or a wild animal in a cage, both of which I felt great empathy with at the moment. It was crazy, all right. Standing there in the middle of the night railing against editors and critics I didn't even have. But there was a thread of reason governing my thinking. Quality is a very subjective notion; quantity is not. If you have to choose between the two, I figured, always go with quantity. The quality may or may not ever be there, but the chances are that only some bitter, failed writer-turned-critic will ever claim to know the difference. You can't write a novel if you're riddled with self-doubt. Indeed, the quality most precious to an author is the *absence of self-doubt*. It doesn't really matter how talented you are. If you hear a voice in your head saying, "No one's going to like this. No one's going to get this," you're probably never going to complete a novel. You could be Oscar Wilde behind bars with your hair on fire but if you're riddled with self-doubt, it may be time to look for another line of work. It may be time to think about becoming a critic.

I sipped the reheated coffee, lit another cigarette, and reflected upon the paradox I was facing. The two people who now most vibrantly populated my life were advising me to take radically different directions regarding the writing of this novel. Clyde felt strongly that I simply should not write it for reasons she'd previously intimated. Fox, on the other hand, felt that writing the novel was vital to my own organic needs. It was like having an angel on one shoulder and a devil on the other, each whispering their wise sibilance into my ears. And how did I feel about it? For the first time in almost seven years, I couldn't have stopped writing this novel if I'd wanted to, and I didn't want to. Hell, as novels go, I'd only just started. Maybe, I thought, I could write it clandestinely, without Clyde's knowledge. But that wasn't going to be easy considering Clyde's ability to make educated guesses, or read minds. At least she appeared to be able to read *mine*.

But it wasn't just the novel that was keeping me up all night. It was Fox's revelation about the circumstances of how and where he'd first met Clyde. There was something almost spiritually incestuous about Fox and Clyde, I now realized. It would be quite a task to determine who was the mentor and who the protégé. Even more important, who was telling the truth to poor, lonely Walter Snow? Was Clyde a fraud? Had she lied to me about everything she'd ever told me? Or was her claim to have told fortunes in a carnival merely a quite understandable cover story for someone who didn't want her nefarious, drug-addicted past to become known? Should I confront her with it or just play along for a while?

With my recently written fictional sexual encounter still redolent in the room, it was time, I felt, to question both of them about their living arrangements and their loving arrangements. It was odd, I thought, that I still hadn't deciphered the true nature of their relationship. Yet, suppose I got differing stories from the two of them? Which one should I believe? Were they partners in some kind of open marriage? Was this the beginning of some kind of sordid love triangle? Was it the beginning of Walter Snow making a fool of himself? Or had that started long before I'd ever met Clyde and Fox? I simply did not know the answers to these questions and yet I needed them desperately if I was ever going to finish the novel.

You might ask, if a novel is a work of fiction, why would I necessarily need to know the truth about Fox and Clyde? The answer is a closely guarded secret that very few authors ever deign to share with their readers. But I see no reason not to share it with you now. And yet, I'm hesitant to reveal any trade secrets, just as any good magician or detective never likes to explain his tricks or articulate his methodology. But what the hell? What on earth could I possibly have to lose? You've probably guessed the secret by now anyway. Why did I so passionately require the truth? *Because all great fiction is true.*

You see? That's why Houdini and Sherlock never revealed their methods. Because the moment they did, everyone on the planet would say, "I knew that!" And the next thing they would say is "I could've done that!" But they didn't know that and they *couldn't* have done that. (This does not apply, of course, to fortune-tellers at carnivals.)

CHAPTER 17

Despite the emotional turmoil I was experiencing concerning Clyde's relationship with Fox and my relationships with them, I was not at all prepared for what took place the following night at the Old Armory. I don't know what it was I'd expected actually. Maybe a soup-kitchen kind of thing where normal Americans like myself, with the help of Donald Trump's credit card, of course, served dinner to the homeless. Whatever I'd expected, I'd been wrong in at least two principal areas: I'd underestimated Clyde and Fox's abilities to pursue their "little" hobbies, and, like most well-intentioned but severely sheltered people, I'd underestimated the true nature of the plight of the homeless. Having mentioned these two caveats, these lapses in my knowledge of the human condition, I can truthfully say that a good time was had by all, if only for a night.

If you've never been to a homeless shelter, maybe you should go. Or maybe you shouldn't. It is not likely to be the kind of thing you will ever be liable to forget. Possibly it was the contrast between the place itself and the events that took *place* there that has created, even after all this time, such an indelible impression upon my mind. (It is quite a challenge for any author to convey in mere words the squalor and the nobility of the race of man. In a sense, the author's work is rather simple: ordering and reordering phrases and sentences; pushing words around like a seriously ill Scrabble player; transfiguring people and events and emotions onto the feckless page in such a manner that the reader, having read, will become so involved in the illusion of life itself that he will forget, for all practical purposes, that he is, indeed, reading a book. That is the author's sacred task and it is one I do not for a moment casually embrace. But simply willing a powerful effect upon the reader does not make it so. It requires a talent that is almost effortless, virtually invisible, and that is the rarest talent of all. Every author worth reading must do his best even as he struggles with success, as if he's typing with his toes or merely paying the rent, to not inflict his own life upon the lives of his characters. The reader must observe the book's greatness almost peripherally, as the author, in the dark of the night, repositions his little words and phrases like chess pieces until he makes life appear so real that he dies trying. When all is said and done, as an author, all you can really ever do is pray to the gods to give you one good line. Then all you can do is pray for another one after that and another one after that.)

The night before the "event" at the Old Armory,

a limo was sent to pick me up at my apartment. I was looking out my window when it arrived and it was so long and so black that it practically obliterated the rather pathetic, periscopic view the basement window provided. Clyde had called earlier to tell me, in hurried, businesslike tones, that tonight would be sort of a "scouting party" to check the place out before the real party on the following night.

"I think it might be a good idea," she'd said, "for you to acclimate yourself to the place before the big night."

"Okay," I'd said, "but—"

"In the history of Western civilization," she'd continued, "you may be the first person to ever arrive at this particular address in a black stretch limo. Fox and I regard you very highly, Walter."

"Okay," I'd said, "but is the limo really necessary?"

"Is homelessness really necessary?" she'd replied. Then she'd hung up.

Now I was in the limo heading over to the armory on Sixty-seventh Street, on the east side. Blocks and blocks of nighttime Manhattan slipped almost soundlessly past my window. People on the sidewalks were still going nowhere quickly. Some of them noticed my black stretch limo but most of them were too busy going nowhere. At least I had a destination and a means, if somewhat lavish, of getting there. This limo, I realized, was just a part of another one of Clyde's little hobbies. And wherever I was going was merely the next amusement for her and her dear friend Fox, who'd been in and out of prisons and mental hospitals and homeless shelters and had recently imparted the information to me that Clyde had been a heroin addict.

And why should her past disturb me? Nobody's proud of being a heroin addict so she'd just concocted some ridiculous story about meeting Fox when the carnival left town. It had a better ring to it than telling someone that you'd met your roommate at a heroin rehab program in Arizona. And again I wondered, as I watched Manhattan slipping by like somebody else's sordid dream, why should it bother me? Had I been secretly imagining white picket fences safely surrounding Clyde and myself? Had I been subconsciously scheming to make an honest woman of her? Would the fact that she might be a psychopathic liar and a heroin addict get in the way of my plans? Or could love conquer all? It never had yet, I reflected grimly. I did not much like these backseat-of-limo ruminations. It was a good thing, I thought, that I didn't employ this mode of transportation often. It was a smooth ride but it tended to be a bit hard on your dreams.

It was after ten o'clock by the time the long black limo pulled up like an urban shark in front of a large, old, somehow slightly foreboding structure. The driver got out and opened the door for me. He touched his cap rather a bit

151

too deferentially, I thought. Maybe he hated me.

"Do I owe you a tip?" I asked.

"Oh, no, sir," he replied. "Mr. Trump has hired this limo for the next forty-eight hours. The tip's included."

Mr. Trump, my ass, I thought. Trump didn't get to be Trump by being a chump. How could Clyde think she could possibly get away with this? I was now becoming quite ambivalent about her judgment. She had some balls all right but she'd chosen a pretty big enemy to pick a fight with. When Trump got wind of this credit-card scam, we could all wind up in the calaboose without a sucker like Walter Snow to fork over our bail.

Fox met me on the steps, embracing me warmly, pushing the one-hitter under my nose, seemingly in great spirits. Fox always had an infectious happiness about him, especially when he was happy. He did not need to twist my arm to get me to take a deep hit off the little device.

"Just what you need to brace you up a bit," he said. "Have you ever been inside a large homeless shelter in New York?"

"I'm afraid I haven't," I said.

"Then you're just like most other New Yorkers. They're so absorbed in their own problems that they walk right past hell on earth every day and night and they don't even know it. But you'll be different soon. Nobody walks in here and walks out again the same person, unless, of course, you happen to be homeless. Now tomorrow night you're not even going to recognize this place. But tonight, well, you'll see. Welcome to the armory!"

Fox took me up the steps and through the doors into the big old structure that, he explained, was over a hundred years old and used to be an enormous staging area for training men and horses before World War I. I gazed around at what must have been forty-foot ceilings. It was hard to imagine there being this much space in New York.

"The place is no longer operated by the military," Fox was saying, "but it still preserves all of the old institutional flavor. Maybe more so now. Here, I'll show you."

He opened another door and suddenly an overpowering stench affronted our senses, not unlike what I imagined to be the smell of a mass grave. We entered a long room that was full of row upon row of pathetic little mental-hospital steel cots, barely the width of a normal human body. It looked, indeed, like something out of a fairy tale gone awry, and maybe that's what it was.

"At this time of year," Fox said, "when the weather is cold, there's rarely an empty cot. The building sleeps fifteen hundred to two thousand men, and the cops are bringing more in all the time. They sleep in their clothes, of course. What they have on their bodies is usually about all they have in the world. Lights out is at eleven. As you can see, most of them are already asleep on their little cots."

"Jesus," I said. "They look like rows and rows of little elves."

"That's a very good description, Walter. But then, again, you *are* an author and we've come to expect these kinds of insights from you."

As always, it was difficult to tell whether Fox was complimenting me or patronizing me and I decided for better or worse just to let it go. It was merely one man's observation about another man's observation. It would take two shrinks to get to the bottom of Fox's brand of mental gymnastics and, from what Clyde had told me, many more than two shrinks had already tried.

"You'll notice," Fox was saying, "that just about every man here, while sleeping in his clothes, has taken his shoes off."

"That would be hard to miss," I said.

"I've seen a few more of these places than I'd like to admit, and in all that time I've never gotten used to the smell. That's one way to demarcate the truly homeless from the mere jet-set gypsies like myself. If you notice the smell, there's still a chance for you. If you no longer notice it, you're a true no-hoper."

A true no-hoper, I thought to myself. If ever there was a good phrase to have met an author's eager ear, this was it. There was no question that I would use the phrase and many others of Fox's in the novel. An author or an actor invariably resorts to the ongoing vampirization of his friends, if, indeed, he has any friends, which is not always the case. To an author at work, every friend, acquaintance, lover, and casual stranger is a victim waiting to be raped and pillaged for everything about them of human worth. In this instance, Fox, albeit unwittingly, had delivered a fine phrase to my war chest of words. A true no-hoper, I thought. That was a keeper.

"Take it," said Fox, with his maddening, not to say frightening, ability to see to the very depths of my being. "It's yours."

We walked in silence for a while down the endless rows of little cots filled with the detritus of the human race, filled with broken American dreams. We came to a point in the middle of the vast room at which Fox signaled me to stop. He put his hand up.

"Listen, Walter," he half whispered. "Do you hear that sound?"

There was the muffled street noise that was always in New York, from the swankiest hotel to the saddest shelter. You had to screen it out and, like not noticing the smell in the armory, if you no longer heard the street noise, you could say you were a true New Yorker. I made my mind listen intently and then I heard it. It sounded like an engine or a motor of some kind coming from no fixed point and from everywhere at the same time. At moments it sounded like a dissonant note and at others the noise appeared to be a not-unattractive layering of harmonic tones. It was, I realized at last, the oddly heartbreaking sound of over a thousand homeless men snoring.

"It's a regular human symphony, isn't it, Walter? The sounds of all these men snoring, coughing, burping, murmuring, calling out some cherished, half-remembered name from long ago, farting. It's a sad symphony, Walter, and very few people ever get a chance to hear it. It's a symphony of the forgotten."

Whatever I'd thought of Fox Harris may have in some unchartable way changed forever at that moment. As so often happens when two men vie for the very same object of affection, neither of us mentioned Clyde. But I could see, possibly clearly for the first time, what Clyde saw in Fox, and, I must confess, even filtered through my own vastly different personal experience, I was quite deeply taken by what I saw.

Before I knew it, Fox had moved perilously close to me and put his arms around me as if we were a couple slow-dancing to a certain celestial music that only we could hear. Maybe it was the effect of the one-hitter. Maybe it was the otherworldly nature of the peaceful, somnolent scene all around us. Maybe it was the knowledge that this person shared an intimacy with a person I'd only loved, only fantasized, only written about from afar. Whatever the reason, I did not push Fox away from me though we stood together very close for some moments in that strange and shabby ballroom of the spirit. One voice inside me told me to go with the flow because it would bring me ever closer to Clyde. But another voice whispered wickedly something equally close to the truth. Do not repulse this person's advances, it said. Don't you understand that he is a man after your own heart? Probably the embrace lasted only a moment but it would alter always the way I looked at Fox and perhaps even the way I would look at life. He took my hand as if nothing had happened and we walked a little farther down the rows of little men snoring in their little beds.

"Do you see," said Fox, "how most of them have placed one shoe under each front bedpost of their cots?"

It was strange, I thought, that I hadn't noticed it before. Maybe I hadn't noticed a lot of things before. But it was a strange night in a strange world and I could see quite vividly now the images of these men protecting their worn-out, pathetic, common labor shoes, which no one in the city of New York would ever walk a mile in, from being stolen by another no-hoper. It said as much or as little about human beings, I felt, as any of us would ever want to know.

"The cots, of course, will all be moved aside tomorrow night. Clyde is going so ape shit with this thing that for the first time, maybe even Donald Trump may have some trouble keeping up with his credit-card expenditures. It's going to be the party to end all parties, I can tell you. Do you recognize this fine stalwart specimen over here?"

157

I followed Fox over to a corner where two cots had been pulled together side by side to accommodate the slumbering form of one of the largest black men I'd ever seen before. And, yes, I had seen him before. It was Teddy.

"Tomorrow night is his big night," said Fox, "and he doesn't even know it yet. He's going to be more than merely the guest of honor. Tomorrow night is going to be his coronation! He's going to be crowned, in his head, king of an imaginary African nation! How many of us poor devils will ever get to realize and achieve that lofty a goal in our lives?"

I gazed down at the sleeping form of Teddy and was suddenly taken with how very childlike, how incredibly angelic he appeared. In the midst of all the sorrow and sadness and squalor and suffering and shabbiness that so invaded and permeated this enormous, god-awful hall slept this giant of a man with a face like a child. The look of peace on that face was the next best thing to being dead, I thought.

"When they dream," said Fox, "they go to the same places we do."

CHAPTER 18

I hadn't seen Clyde since the night at the Unicorn when we'd stood bathed in the celestial light of the jukebox and she'd given me a kiss I will probably never forget. Fox was still in jail then and I was still green enough to believe almost everything either of them told me. Looking back on that time, I realize it was almost childish of me to have thought that what was true and what was false were two separate, disparate, distinctive entities. I have learned since then, a tip of the hat to Clyde and Fox on this one, I suppose, that what is literally true or false has nothing to do whatsoever with the deeper, greater, and sacred truths that drive the green fuses of the flowers and govern all the hearts of man. I missed seeing Clyde very much. It was painful for me to be out of touch with her. I felt almost like, excuse the simile, a heroin addict going through withdrawal. One day, I resolved, I would discover the truth, the real truth, about Clyde and Fox: who they were, what they were, what they meant to each other. One day I would also no doubt discover what the two of them had meant to my lonely, insular life. In the meantime, I vowed, live with them and love with them as much as I humanly was able. I would let them be Clyde and Fox. This was the moral high road, of course, and that road is always the road less traveled. Had I maintained my promise to myself and stayed on that road, they would both undoubtedly be in my life today. But in the nonfiction world where we live, hearts are often broken and lives are routinely destroyed, and whoever or whatever is left must scurry with only the clothes on our backs and the shoes held in place under our bedposts to the world of fiction where no one and nothing can ever harm us.

I'd spent most of the night before, after I'd returned from the armory, writing, and now I was bathed in that pleasant afterglow known in the literary community as "having written." I was getting fairly close, however, to the time, in the early afternoon usually, when the familiar, nagging elbow in the ribs would come along, reminding me that it was almost time to start writing again. It was, to compound a poor simile by repeating it, a bit like being a heroin addict. If you didn't write on a regular basis, you suffered for it. I wondered if Clyde had indeed been a heroin addict or was it just possible that, in order to cool my ardor for her or maybe just out of spite, Fox had invented that rather troubling background for her. I wanted to know and yet I didn't really want to know. I wanted to love Clyde without reservation, without barriers, in a spirit of purity for who she was.

Thinking of Clyde again reminded me that I had done little if anything to pursue the "wankers" who had been harassing our friend Jonjo at the Unicorn. I was not a detective. Hell, I wasn't even a very prolific writer. But I found the business card Jonjo had given me in the pocket of my coat and decided to try my hand at a little sleuthing. I needed to have something to tell Clyde just in case she asked me about it tonight. I could always make it up, of course. People made up stuff every day. That's how politicians stay in office. That's how marriages stay together. That's how novels get written. But it's always nice when you can hang what you believe to be a piece of fiction upon what you believe to be a thread of truth.

It was late morning now, the day of Teddy's big coronation, which I looked forward to as much for the chance to hang out with Clyde as anything else. I poured a cup of fresh coffee and studied Stanton Malowitz's business card as if it contained some deep secret regarding the meaning of life. To help Clyde with this latest amusement of hers was the least I could do. After all, it might have meant the world to Jonjo, but whatever happened to the Unicorn did not really impinge upon my life in any significant way. The only things I seemed to care about lately were the novel and its two principal characters. I sipped the coffee, picked up the phone, and punched in the number on Stanton Malowitz's business card.

"Northwest Properties," said the receptionist's impassive voice.

"Stanton Malowitz, please," I said.

"He's away on business, sir. Can I take a message?"

"Do you know when he'll be back?"

"I have no idea, sir."

"Maybe you can help me then. Where is this area code that I'm calling?"

"It's Seattle, sir," said the receptionist. She appeared to be running out of charm.

"And this is a real estate office?"

"This is Northwest Properties, sir. You'll have to speak with Mr. Malowitz if you want more information."

"But he gave me this card," I said, fabricating a trivial piece of fiction. A writer of fiction needs to keep in practice.

"I'm sure he did, sir. Would you care to leave a message?"

"Yes. But can you tell me something? Just exactly what does Northwest Properties do? Whom do they represent?"

"Sir," said the receptionist, beginning to vent a slight irritation with the caller, "you'll have to speak with Mr. Malowitz."

"And you don't know when he'll be back?"

"No, sir. Is that all, sir?"

I left the woman my name and number and I hung up the phone but I definitely felt something wasn't quite kosher here. If I'd been more alert,

I might have seen what is sometimes called a red flag. But I wasn't an amateur sleuth and I wasn't writing a detective novel (except, of course, in the sense that all good novels are in some fashion detective novels, or at least mystery novels. The real mystery is how they are created, what ingredients are used, and how in the world a writer himself hasn't a clue as to where his life is going). I was, however, slightly put off by the tone and timbre of the receptionist at Northwest Properties. I'd always understood that real estate outfits were extremely customer friendly, eager for clients and business of all manner. The woman I had talked to sounded almost defensive. Strange, I thought. Passing strange. But stranger things, indeed, were about to happen.

The big black stretch limo picked me up again early that evening and drove me out to the Old Armory. A curtain of dark gray was coming down over the city and by the time I got there, the building itself seemed to somehow blend into the melancholy milieu. The driver tipped his cap again and I walked up the weatherbeaten old steps without seeing a sign of life, homeless or otherwise. Maybe I had the wrong night, I thought. Or the wrong lobby. Or maybe I had the wrong hobby. Then I opened the big wooden door and I couldn't believe my eyes. The place looked, at least at first glance, like a fancy ballroom scene from *Dr. Zhivago*.

Long tables with white linen tablecloths stretched

across the big hall as far as the eye could see. Banners and streamers and elaborate floral arrangements were everywhere. If you didn't look too closely, the affair had the appearance of a lavish wedding or possibly an upscale bar mitzvah. There were waiters in tuxedos bearing food on silver trays. An entire orchestra was tuning up on the far side of the room. It was a gala event all right, by any standard. There was so much noise and excitement in the air, in fact, that I was taken quite aback when I felt a pair of child-size but definitely womanly hands cupped over my eyes from behind me.

"Guess who, Sunshine!" a voice shouted above the din.

"Sylvia Plath?"

"Guess again, Walter."

"Mother Teresa?"

"Guess again, you bastard."

"Well, let me see. Since there are over a thousand *men* here—"

"Over *two* thousand—"

"—and of the only two women I saw, one was playing a harp and the other was carrying a tray of caviar, it appeared. That leaves only the gorgeous, fun-loving, irreplaceable—"

"Keep going, Sunshine."

"—woman I love, Clyde."

And then she turned me around and suddenly she was in my arms, her hands caressing the back of my neck, kissing me hotly, just as the orchestra started to play.

"Care to dance?" she said when she came up for air.

"I never learned the bossa nova," I said.

"Never mind. We'll dance later. But, Sunshine, look around you! We really pulled it off! We did it!"

I looked around admiringly. I wasn't exactly sure what it was that we'd done. There was a man with no teeth trying to eat a lobster. There were other men ferociously devouring caviar with their fingers. There was a man who looked like Rumpelstiltskin throwing up his toenails in a silver punch bowl. Two men were fighting over a leg of lamb. Another man was urinating on the floor, off to the side where a klezmer band was starting to warm up. I didn't know it, but things were going to get a lot worse before the coronation of King Teddy would ever get off the blocks. Clyde, of course, was totally oblivious to all this and seemed to be in a state of great euphoria. Whether she was happy because hungry men were eating or whether it was because she'd scammed Trump into unknowingly picking up the tab, I did not know. Very possibly, it was a combination of the two. The men were definitely putting away a lot of food and the cuisine was of a decidedly lavish nature.

"Isn't it wonderful!" she exclaimed. "Some of these men probably haven't eaten in a week and now they're dining on caviar, truffles, lobster, and leg of lamb."

"I don't know if 'dining' is the operative word here," I said.

Clyde did not seem to hear me. I looked at her eyes all asparkle and her stunning, crooked smile and, in the admittedly brief time I'd known her, I'd never seen her appear to be so happy. It was a strange road to happiness, I thought, and many of us, including myself, often got lost along the way. Who was I to impugn her little hobbies? Many of them were illegal, of course, but they did seem to skew toward favoring the poor, the downtrodden, the underdog, and that rarest of all commodities, justice, which, if left to God and the law seems to be dispensed only in an arbitrary, haphazard, and sometimes downright perverse fashion. Who was I to condemn Clyde? I, who loved her. I, who'd become a vegetarian and accomplice in crime because of her. I, who needed strength that I wasn't sure she had. I, who needed and stole her for a work of fiction. My reflections, such as they were, were suddenly brought to a halt by a sharp pounding on the back and I turned to see Fox Harris, who looked as reckless and exhilarated as a drunken sailor on his last night of shore leave.

"Party's only starting, Walter," he shouted above the din. "Wait'll you see what happens next!"

What happened next was fairly predictable since, according to Fox, he'd taken twenty-four cases of Dom Pérignon and poured them into the large yellow plastic water barrels that ringed the hall. Alcohol, of course, was not permitted in the shelter. Tonight, however, was a special night and, again, according to Fox, absolutely nothing had been spared.

Before our eyes, the scene began to degenerate at a staggeringly rapid pace. Fights broke out up and down the banquet hall. Tables were overturned. Men were puking and pissing and coughing their guts out and singing and dancing. And, like its counterpart on the *Titanic*, the orchestra continued to play. The feverish scene, and Fox's and Clyde's reaction to it, are things I will never forget. And, like the orchestra, I played along.

"Now I'd like to dance," said Clyde.

"Are you crazy?" I blurted out.

She looked at me then in the strangest way and I instantly regretted the remark. It's very hard to abandon the person you've always been and it takes some of us longer than others.

"I hope so," she said.

She took my hand. I held her close to me. And we danced.

It was good while it lasted but it didn't last long. Fox cut in. Then a guy who looked like he could be Jack the Ripper. Then half a dozen homeless men in succession who, I have to say, looked to the untrained eye pretty much like what we used to call bums. Then the orchestra took a break, the klezmer band unleashed its own brand of dervishlike music, and the whole scene descended, if possible, even further into chaos and madness. By the time Teddy walked regally into the hall, fully prepped by Fox for his grand coronation, the place looked like the French Revolution had hit it at a hundred miles an hour.

Before anybody knew it, Teddy had made his way up to a podium and was majestically striving to silence the klezmer band, which was no small feat if you've ever had a close encounter with a klezmer band. Teddy wore purple robes, and on the way to the podium, Fox had caught up with the striding monarch just in time to place a gleaming crown of gold upon his head. There was something vaguely Christlike about the whole operation, but I wasn't sure what it was. Maybe it was Fox hurriedly placing the crown upon his head. Maybe it was just the idea of feeding the starving multitudes. Or maybe it was the simple spirit of goodwill toward his fellow man that always seemed to emanate from this large homeless creature called Teddy.

"He even *looks* like a king!" said Clyde excitedly. "Fox got those robes out of his closet."

"I didn't realize Fox had a closet," I said.

Clyde started to say something else but the klezmer band had now ceased operations and Teddy's voice could be heard booming with resonance and purpose throughout the great hall.

"My loyal subjects," he began. "It is with great humility that I accept the burden of the throne. As you may well know, I have in the past been one of you and now I will strive unceasingly to promote your health, education, and welfare in my new role as your king."

The response to this magnanimous statement was less than overwhelming. Indeed, it seemed not dissimilar to the sound of one hand clapping. In addition, Teddy's subjects did not much resemble a tribe of Masai warriors. Many of them, apparently, had made a few too many visits to the Dom Pérignon barrels and were now mumbling incoherently to themselves, panhandling other panhandlers, or passed out in their goose pâtés. None of this, however, appeared to derail Teddy's zealotry.

"You may well ask," he continued, "who is this new King Teddy? What does he stand for? Thus, I will tell you now, my loyal subjects, exactly what I, King Teddy, stand for. I stand for fireworks on the Fourth of July! I stand for the virtuous pursuit of keeping my place in a line for a free hot meal! I stand for the purpose of stretching my legs after too long a period of sitting on my ass! I stand for hemorrhoidal relief! I stand for the chance to gladly give my place on the subway to a person more weary than myself! I stand for bridges and beans and booze and memories and hopes and dreams and handouts and hand-me-downs and happiness and cigarettes and Good Samaritans and friendly whores and fat, easygoing cops and leftovers and stray dogs and stray cats and strays in general and park benches and Indian summers and redemption and salvation for every soul in pain! I stand for a better view of the spectacle of life! I stand for all these things, my loyal subjects, and for much, much more, because every time I stand, I stand for the dignity of man!"

Unfortunately, very few in the hall appeared to be listening to Teddy's words. But I could see that Fox was. And Clyde, I noticed, was standing in rapt attention with tears in her eyes. And, I suppose, you could say that I, too, was listening. The problem was simply that then, as now, I knew that I didn't stand for anything.

CHAPTER 19

It isn't that difficult for two soulful, mercurial individuals to come along and take over your life, especially if you don't have a life. Or at least if you didn't really have one until they came into it.

Now you suddenly find yourself swept mightily along by currents that flow from places you know not and go to places beyond your imagination. It is not an unpleasant feeling to tumble off the wagon and into the arms of your comrades as you leave the passing parade far behind and learn new ways of looking at things, new feelings you didn't know you could have, and new and exciting hobbies that might very well destroy the world as you know it. But you never really knew it, did you? That's the whole point, I guess. Unless you write it down on paper, it sounds as if you're telling it all to a shrink or something. The truth is, of course, it's fun to be out of control until the shit hits the fan. By then, unfortunately, you've lost whatever nonlife you never had in the first place.

What truly seemed to be anchoring my existence at this time was the fact that I was writing the novel. Events in the casino of fiction, indeed, were hurtling by at a far greater pace than any world progress I'd ever witnessed from my basement window. The novel, incredibly, was taking on a life of its own and, in so doing, was taking me along with it for the ride of a lifetime. There were times, of course, like the period immediately following Teddy's coronation, that I had to virtually type like a madman in the night in order to capture in words the events of the previous day. At times like those, I wrote like a man with his hair on fire, like Oscar Wilde behind bars, to do poetic justice to what was the reality of my experience. At other times, the Land of Counterpane was a far friendlier, more facile place than the world in which we all inhabit. My relationship with Clyde, for instance, was a great deal more intimate in fiction than in actuality. But somehow I managed to remain myself in both areas. I suppose you could say that was my saving grace, if in the end I was actually able to save any. Gracewise, it was just about as bad an ending as you could imagine. The novel itself ended rather cleverly, I thought. In real life and in fiction, in fact, the author came out relatively unscathed by subsequent events. The other characters, both on the page and off, I regret to say, did not fare nearly as well. I do not blame myself for what happened, however. I leave the assessment of blame, as all fiction writers must eventually do, to God and small children.

Two nights after Teddy's grand coronation party, the three principal troublemakers gathered for a cheerful little postmortem celebration at the Unicorn. The place was uncharacteristically packed that night and we proceeded to drink our way through a rolling, smooth brown ocean of Guinness in a very short period of time. If it hadn't been for my two central characters, Clyde Potts and Fox Harris, I reflected as I glanced around the seedy, crowded bar, I wouldn't have been drinking and I wouldn't have been writing. In an odd way, I thought, the two of them had saved my life as well as my career. I never really got to thank them for it, but when you think about it, how can you thank people for being themselves? Also, I said to myself, if the flesh-and-blood Clyde and Fox hadn't run into Walter Snow, they never would have passed into the hallowed casino of fiction in the first place. By the time our little trinity had become undone, however, there would be more than enough gratitude and more than enough blame to go around. Their lives, of course, would be ruined and my career would be established, but believe me, I did not know this as we sat in the Unicorn cheerfully, hopefully, obliviously toasting each other that fateful night.

"Never above you," said Clyde, standing up and toasting Fox and myself simultaneously. She held her Guinness slightly higher than ours as we clinked glasses. Fox and I exchanged rather quizzical glances.

"Never below you," said Clyde, this time holding her glass slightly lower than Fox's and mine.

"Always by your side," said Clyde, clinking her glass square on with the two of us. We drained our pints and Fox put his arms around Clyde and she put her arms around me and the three of us stood there in an intimate circle with our arms around each other in the middle of the crowded little bar. It was a moment to savor, and moments, according to Fox, were the vessels for great and beautiful things. According to Fox, that's why they lasted forever.

"Sunshine," said Clyde. "Should we say hello to Jonjo?"

"Sure," I said. "If we can find him."

It was true that Jonjo was barely visible to the naked eye. The leprechaun was totally obscured by customers crowding around the little bar.

"Business looks good," said Clyde. "What did you find out about those wankers Jonjo was so worried about?"

"Well," I said, "I have done a bit of detective work but so far I've run into a brick wall. I got Jonjo to give me a business card from one of his enemies—who could be completely imaginary, it's always a possibility. Anyway, I called this guy named Stanton Malowitz at a company called Northwest Properties. They're based in Seattle. But I must say, they did not sound like any real estate company I've ever dealt with."

"You think it's a front for something?" asked Fox, eager not to be left out of anything.

"It's certainly possible," I said. "The woman was almost dismissive of me. More than anything, she seemed to want to protect Malowitz from anybody contacting him. It was strange. I thought those kinds of outfits would be very client friendly. I thought they always tried to keep the customer satisfied."

"Keeping the customer satisfied went out with the buggy whip," said Fox rather cynically. "That's the way big corporations do business these days."

"Maybe," said Clyde. "Still, it *is* strange."

"Maybe I'll go to the men's room," said Fox. "Me and a little bit of Malabimbi Madness."

"Maybe I'll come along," I said.

"Maybe I'll go over and try to see Jonjo," said Clyde.

"Maybe you'll need a periscope," said Fox, as the two of us got up and headed for the head.

The place was packed tighter than a can of smoked oysters, which was odd for the Unicorn on a weeknight. I wondered about it as I followed Fox's lanky form threading its way through the crowd to the men's room. Once I'd gotten in the can with Fox, bolted the door, and had a few rounds with the one-hitter, I didn't think anything more about it. As usual, I didn't think anything more about anything.

"Got a smoke?" said Fox.

"A smoke?" I asked.

"Yes, Walter, a smoke. A cigarette."

"Oh, a cigarette."

I fished for my pack of Camels, gave one to Fox, and lit it for him. He took a few puffs.

"This is a smoke," he said.

Then he opened the heart-shaped silver locket again and ground the tip of the one-hitter into its dark brown contents. I lit him up again and he took a deep pull from the cigarette that wasn't really a cigarette.

"Now *this*," he said, "is the smoke of life. It can help you lose yourself or it can help you find yourself or it can help you find out what is, or what is not, or what ought to be."

"Interesting," I said, watching Fox's eyes spin like roulette wheels and sparkle like stars.

"For instance," he said, "it just came to me here in the men's room what is really happening here at the Unicorn tonight. Why there's such a crowd here. What it truly feels like."

"What does it truly feel like?"

"A fucking wake," said Fox.

"A wake?"

"Exactly. A wake for the Unicorn. Everybody's upbeat and full of drunken cheer and nobody's talking about it but I'll bet they all know. I'll bet those guys you were talking about have finally fat-armed Jonjo out of here. I knew something was slightly off when we walked in, but it was just like if you walk into a wake at a certain time you can't tell if it's a party or a wake and maybe that's the point of it all. I didn't know for sure until I came in this men's room and took a few hits of the smoke of life. That's what told me there was death in the air."

"Wow," I said. It was all I could think to say. Was the Unicorn really going belly-up tonight? Was it possible that one could take a few hits of Malabimbi Madness and suddenly gain the insights into a situation that Fox had just espoused to me? What he'd said had certainly had the ring of truth. Now if I could just manage to navigate my way back to the table.

Fox and I fairly floated out of the men's room and I followed him, weaving this way and that through the human tapestry until we saw Clyde sitting alone at the table with her head down on her folded arms. She looked up and I could see that her eyeliner or eye shadow or whatever women wear was running and she'd been crying.

"You look like Alice Cooper," said Fox.

"I *feel* like Alice Cooper," she said. "Jonjo's going out of business tonight. All drinks are on the house. By tomorrow morning, the Unicorn will be extinct."

After a little more encouragement and another round of Guinness, Clyde revealed a few more details about her conversation with Jonjo. She seemed to be taking the matter a lot harder than I would have expected. Indeed, she seemed to be taking it almost personally.

"Isn't there anything we can do?" she wailed. "Jonjo introduced me to his wife, Moira. She was crying, too. She put her arms around me though she'd never seen me in her life and we both cried. She said the health department and about three other city agencies seem to have gotten together and decided that vast changes must be made immediately and they just can't afford to do it. She also said Jonjo had told her that the landlord has suddenly decided to quadruple the rent, starting next month."

"It does seem like a concerted effort to get them out of here," Fox said.

"Isn't there anything we can do?" Clyde wailed again. "I don't want the only Unicorn in New York City to disappear forever."

We looked over at the bar at this point and Jonjo, appearing more leprechaunlike than ever, gave us all a heartbreaking little good-bye wave. It was a poignant moment and it started up the waterworks again for Clyde.

"Can't we pull out Trump's credit card for one last hurrah?" I asked.

"No chance," said Clyde. "The bastard cut us off."

"Some people," said Fox.

I knew in my heart, of course, that Trump's money was Trump's money and that it did not in any way belong to us. I knew full well that what we had done was not only a little hobby. In legal terms, it was a felony. I knew as well that life was unfair, that some are born to sweet delight and some are born to endless night. But all these notions had apparently gotten mixed up in my mind and by the time they reached what I like to think of as my conscience the only message they seemed to deliver was that it was okay to steal Donald Trump's money. In fact, anything we did was okay. For all practical purposes, I suppose, you could say that my conscience had been left at the dry cleaner's.

The crowd was thinning out a bit but the Guinness kept flowing and the mood of our little trio began to get increasingly reckless and fatalistic. I was just on my way back to the table from another trip to the men's room with Fox when I noticed Clyde staring intently at the far wall of the place.

"I don't believe it!" she exclaimed, an expression of total incredulity on her face.

"I don't either," said Fox. "Now what exactly is it that we don't believe?"

"Trump is on the local news," she said, pointing to the television set high up against the wall. "They're interviewing him about our gala at the armory."

As if drawn by a magnet, the three of us moved quickly to a spot as close to the television as we could get. Trump's big head was smiling and speaking to the camera.

"It's just something I've always wanted to do," he was saying. "I saw the opportunity to help those less fortunate than myself."

"Which is just about everybody else," said Fox.

"I wanted to show the homeless in our city that New York does have a big heart," Trump continued. "Maybe it was only for one night, but that night was one that over two thousand homeless people will never forget. Of all the triumphs and accomplishments in my life, the dinner and party for the homeless at the Old Armory two nights ago is one of the acts of which I'm most proud. It is a privilege and a duty to give back to the community—"

"That lying bastard!" screamed Clyde.

"The one-eyed giant strikes again!" shouted Fox. "What a fucking joke! This guy spends his life acquiring casinos and buildings and yachts and then finally when he's forced into a situation in which a charitable act has occurred at his expense he's shameless enough to stand up and take credit for it."

"We couldn't have done it without him," I said, innocently enough.

"Spoken like a true participant-observer of life," said Fox. "What brilliant insights into human nature does our friend the author bring to our table? Of course we couldn't have done it without him. We've always operated strictly on the muldoon. But if it wasn't for fascist capitalistic pigs like him, it probably wouldn't have been necessary to do it in the first place."

"Sunshine," said Clyde. "You know what I want you to bring to our table? Another round of Guinness."

I dutifully got up and walked over to the bar, partly to please Clyde and partly to discourage further scathing diatribes from Fox. Fox, indeed, was beginning to sound like some kind of dinosaur from the sixties. Maybe Gandhi was right. Maybe Trump was wrong. Who gave a shit? Maybe everybody did. I hoped they did because Fox was a central character now. He was important to me in ways he could hardly be expected to know. And, indubitably, Clyde was important. Hell, if you stopped to think about it, even I was important. We were important because we were important to each other. We were all we had. Three star-crossed characters in the book of life.

The high point of the evening for me personally came about twenty minutes later when Clyde, either accidentally or deliberately, spilled half a pint of Guinness directly into my lap, immediately grabbed a few napkins, and began a series of rather excessively elaborate, incredibly zealous, but certainly not unappreciated efforts at mopping up the situation. By this time, of course, all three of us were drunk enough to go duck hunting with a rake. But all that notwithstanding, it was one of those delicious, indelible moments that Fox had alluded to, one of those little moments that will live forever. If you've never had a beautiful woman attempt with all her heart to devotedly, dedicatedly mop up the Guinness she's spilled in your lap, you, my friend, haven't lived.

CHAPTER 20

An old friend of mine once told me that when you're writing a novel, it's all downhill once you get past page fifty-seven. Technically speaking, this is not very professional advice. Indeed, it sounds like the kind of thing a person in a mental hospital might tell you. Nonetheless, I was well past page fifty-seven now and it did seem as if the novel was almost inexorably moving toward its climax, conclusion, and resolution. Was it the great American novel? I frankly doubted it. But it wasn't bad. And no author writing a novel is in any position to assess the quality of his own work. Motivation and ambition are worthless to a writer at this stage. If he believes he's accomplishing great art, toiling at some important work, it rarely turns out to be so. The greatest work in art and literature and music in the recent history of man has almost invariably been produced by people who were just trying to pay the rent.

It was now several days since the night of the closing of the Unicorn. I had not seen or heard from Clyde or Fox since that night and I was beginning to wonder if it had been something I'd said or maybe something I'd written. I was rummaging through the pockets of one of my coats possibly looking for my lost childhood when I came upon a folded slip of paper. The coat, I then realized, was the one I'd worn at the wake for the Unicorn. I opened the slip of paper and found a note written on it in a fine, feminine hand. The note read: "For a good time, call 226–3713." The writer had also included a rather crude, childlike drawing of a broken heart. I was not a great detective or even a detective in any sense of the word, but I did not remember meeting any barflies or even any friendly strangers that night at the Unicorn or any recent night anywhere. My heart, I must report, hoped that the missive had been written and placed in my pocket by Clyde. It was certainly possible, and all I had to do was call the number to find out. But for a reason I do not know, it was not as easy as it sounded. Maybe it was my head telling my heart it was time to play a little hard to get. Or maybe I was feeling guilty about writing the novel in the first place, against Clyde's wishes. Or maybe I was feeling unsure of myself, riddled with self-doubt about the merits of my work. I had been wanting for quite a while to view Clyde and Fox not as what they were, but as what they had become: characters in my novel. Were they compelling? Had I developed them effectively? Had I captured them? There was only one way to find out. I decided that it was finally time to let my former agent and my former editor look over the unfinished manuscript.

Normally, it is not a good idea to let anyone peruse an unfinished manuscript or a work in progress. This time, however, I felt the situation was different. For one thing, I hadn't taken a meeting with either my editor or my agent in almost seven years. For all I knew, they both might now reside in that great publishing house in the sky. Also, to be perfectly honest, I was starting to vacillate rather wildly back and forth between self-congratulation and self-doubt. I needed feedback. I needed input. So that afternoon I took the pages I had down to a nearby Kinko's, made two additional copies, and FedExed them respectively to my agent and my editor. I wrote a brief cover note suggesting that it was urgent that I meet with them as soon as possible. As soon as possible is not very fast for most editors and agents. They tend to believe that responding to matters in a timely fashion is a sign of weakness. If I wanted to meet with them anytime soon, it was not a good policy merely to wait by the phone. I was not proud. If necessary, I planned to barrage and badger both their offices until I got their attention. This is a rather tedious, not to say humbling, aspect of being an author, but once you become a best-seller, of course, *you're* the one who tends to believe that responding to matters in a timely fashion is a sign of weakness. In fact, once you get big and powerful enough, almost everything you do becomes a sign of weakness.

Back at the apartment, I felt a sense of fatalistic calm. I had crossed a professional literary Rubicon of sorts. It now no longer mattered what Clyde thought or what Fox thought or possibly even what I thought. People highly placed inside the industry would very soon be weighing in on things. I poured a cup of coffee and sat down at the typewriter but now I found I could not write. My fingers simply would not move across the keys. I was in full holding-pattern mode until I met with the editor and the agent. It is astonishing how little confidence any of us truly has in our own natural abilities—especially those of us who have determined that fate has called upon us to write. And yet, writing's like chopping wood sometimes, they say. Some of the world's worst writers seem often to excel at chopping wood. Some of the best seem to excel only at lying in the gutter and looking at the stars.

That night, in a state of total creative thought interruptus, there was nothing to do but pace the apartment, go out and get drunk, kill myself, check into a mental hospital, or call Clyde, and I quite sensibly opted for the latter. Judging from her note, she was primed for a good time, and anything was better than waiting in a near-death state of suspended animation to see what the agent and editor had to say about my work. It was very similar to handing in to the teacher something you've worked at very diligently. It was kind of sad to think how little we grow emotionally from the way we felt in the fourth grade.

"Is this the number I call for a good time?" I asked, after hearing Clyde's melodic hello.

"Sunshine!" she said, with the pent-up excitement of a small girl. "I'm so glad you called."

"So am I," I gushed idiotically.

"We've had a lot of good times," she said coyly, "but you and I have never really had a *good time* together. I mean, just the two of us."

I couldn't believe my ears. I couldn't believe how excited I was. I couldn't believe that I suddenly felt like a kid at Christmas.

"The two of us getting together is way over-due," I said.

"I agree, Sunshine."

"Okay. We're on the same wavelength. So is it your place or mine?"

"Mine would be a little difficult. Fox lives here, too, you know. And if I'm not mistaken, he might have a little fit of pique if he caught the two of us between the sheets. What about your place?"

"If you like getting bull-fucked in a basement apartment, it's fine."

"I think we're breaking up."

"I'm not on a cell phone."

"That wasn't what I meant."

There was a silence on the line while we both considered our options. Apparently, I stepped over the line. In a rush of testosterone, in fact, I had very possibly stepped on my dick.

"In a rush of testosterone," I said, "very possibly I've stepped on my dick."

"I like a man who can step on his dick. What I don't like is a man who keeps standing on it."

"I'll keep that in mind."

"Good. Then at least you'll have something on your mind besides the great American novel you were writing."

"Great *Armenian* novel," I said. "And there's no past tense to it. I'm still writing it. In fact, I've already sent copies of the unfinished manuscript to my old editor and my old agent. Later this week I hope to be meeting with both of them."

"Oh, Walter. I want you to write. That's what God, whether you believe in him or not, intended you to do. I just want you to write about something else. Something besides the three of us. What we have is fun and beautiful and real. Relegating us to characters in your novel is like pinning Fox and me to a butterfly board. It will surely destroy what we all have together."

"But Fox *likes* the idea of my writing the novel."

"That's not true. Fox likes you maybe more than you realize, and he wants you to become more of what you are and could be. But he thinks writing about us as characters in a book is very bad karma. He's just too shy to tell you."

"Fox?" I said. "Shy?"

"Maybe you don't know your characters as well as you think you do."

"Look. If it makes you feel better, I can finish

the book then change the names to protect the innocent."

"By the time you finish the book, there won't be any innocence left to protect."

"Surely you're being unrealistic and melodramatic."

"Walter, this may surprise you, but I'm a very private person and so is Fox. We've taken you into our lives with open arms. We've taken you into our hearts. I see things you don't see. I see tragedy if you continue along this path. As a fiction writer, you can write about any subject you choose. You're only limited by your imagination, Walter. Walter, you can write about anything under the sun and I sincerely hope you do, but I'm begging you, for all of our sakes, please don't suck the magic and the humanity out of us to sell to the public. Let Fox and me be what we are. Free birds who choose to be in your sky."

"Ask me anything else and I'll do it for you. I've done everything you've asked of me since the day I met you in the bank and I helped you put the dead fish in the vault."

"You didn't *know* it was a fish."

"That's my point. I trusted you."

"And now you betray me."

"I told you. I'll change the names."

"The only change I care about, Walter, is the change I'm seeing in you."

"What the hell are you trying to do? Destroy my career?"

"Even if that were true, it would be a far better thing than to destroy someone's spirit."

Neither of us said anything for a few moments. Neither of us, I suppose, had anything much left to say. Finally Clyde broke the silence.

"So long, Sunshine," she said.

"So long, Clyde," I said as both of us hung up simultaneously.

We had both done many things together, I thought as I stared at the ceiling. Now we were hanging up together. Saying goodbye together. Suddenly, the ceiling looked very lonely and the room seemed very empty. Then, just as suddenly, there came the silver lining: I was now unhappy enough to become a great writer.

CHAPTER 21

Less than a week later, I walked into the midtown office of my agent, Sylvia Lowell, sat down in the chair in front of her desk, and looked out over the city. Sylvia had a lavish, much-sought-after corner office and the only trouble with the view was that it was one of a great number of large office buildings all teeming with agents in corner offices. I looked into Sylvia's cold obsidian eyes and she looked into mine and, I suppose, neither of us much liked what we saw. She was a power agent who represented a large, rather unwieldy stable of many writers, a small handful of whom were highly successful mainstream wood choppers with only narrow, formulaic talents, and the great mass of whom were unsuccessful, unhappy authors who, though most of them were far more talented than the mainstreamers, spent most of their time silently damning Sylvia Lowell. I don't know how much of it was really her fault. After all, I was a man who hadn't written a book in seven years. All I blamed her for was having cold obsidian eyes.

"The first thing you have to do," she said, "is get rid of that title."

"What's wrong with *The Great Armenian Novel?*" I asked.

"Everything," said Sylvia Lowell. "For starters, it's too inside. It's a book about a book. There's never a market for that."

"Okay," I said. "I'll change the title. How about *The Cat Who Killed Christ?*"

"It's better."

"Well, enough about the title. How'd you like the book?"

Sylvia squinted her eyes slightly, as if she were staring at me through a microscope. I did my best to look like an interesting specimen.

"What happened to you, Walter?" she said at last. "You had so much promise."

I didn't have an answer to that so I didn't give her one. Besides, I didn't know what had happened to me.

"Your first book exhibited such a marvelous economy of words. And the characters practically leaped off the page. And there was a beginning, a middle, and an end. And there was action. Lots of action. *The Rise and Fall of Nothing at All.* Now *there* was a title!"

I waited patiently. It did not bode particularly well that all she'd talked about so far was my previous book. Maybe she was stalling because she hadn't read the pages I'd sent. Of course, you don't have to really read a manuscript to get a sense of it. You just have to know how to read between the lines. Maybe Sylvia had done just that and hadn't loved what she'd read. It was a little like the way George Bernard Shaw had operated in his heyday. He contended that he was such an intuitive genius that he need not actually have to see a play in order to review it. Was it possible that Sylvia Lowell possessed that rare brand of genius? If so, I pondered, why was she an agent?

"I've read what you've sent of *The Great Armenian Novel*," she said, "and to be quite candid, I'm afraid it is *The Great Armenian Novel*."

She let that information sink in for a moment. I took the opportunity to sink a little lower in my chair.

"The book just doesn't work, Walter. It's far too self-conscious, precious, and introspective. It could almost serve as a primer for how *not* to write a novel. The action is jerky and willful and sporadic, what action there is. There isn't enough to sustain the reader's interest. And further, what action there is seems to strain the bounds of credulity. Placing a dead fish in a bank vault? Falsely accusing a psychiatrist of being a pedophile? Springing a large African-American mental patient who thinks he's the king of an imaginary African nation from a mental hospital? This material could be seen as racist, homophobic, politically incorrect, insensitive, and, well, frankly, unrealistic and ludicrous. It's a stretch for anyone reading this book to believe that people really do these things. It's simply not believable."

"I see."

"No, apparently you don't. It's not just the dearth of action that makes this manuscript so wanting. The characters are developed in a very vexing and peculiar fashion. They seem to spring up out of the earth fully formed, like Greek gods. They are not the kind of characters any reader might readily identify with or empathize with or even care about very much. By the way, are the Clyde and the Fox characters real people?"

"I'm not sure."

"When you find out, let me know. In the meantime, remember, Walter, when you impart something to the page, you invariably unmask yourself. This book may tell us more about your character, the author, than it does about the characters about whom you are supposedly writing. I know I may not sound encouraging, but you know, Walter, that it's my policy never to encourage bad writing even by authors who can do better."

"Unless it sells," I muttered.

"What?"

"Unless it sells!" I practically shouted. "As bad writing so often does. And, Sylvia, this manuscript is a *work in progress*. It's only *half* finished. And it is only a novel in the sense that people may perceive it to be fiction. It's really a totally nonfiction account of the lives of three people in New York, one of which happens to be mine."

"I see," said Sylvia Lowell.

"Apparently, you don't," I said, pressing my

advantage, trivial or imagined as it may have been. "This is a real story about real people. I can't tell you what happens because it hasn't happened yet, but believe me, it's going to. This is not a mystery or a pot-boiler or a romance. It falls into the category of the 'unclassifiable.' And the last time I checked, most of the great art and literature of the past century falls into that category as well. If Mozart, Kafka, or Van Gogh were alive today, they'd probably be living in a homeless shelter, which, by the way, is where my next scene takes place."

"Walter, Walter, Walter," said Sylvia Lowell in what sounded like a rather rueful mantra. "I'm not attacking you. Don't forget that I'm on your side. Whatever I tell you is going to sound sugarcoated compared to the way the critics will undoubtedly savage your work. But you're the writer. Write what you want."

"By the way," I said, "did you hear about the writer who came home one day and found that his house had burned down, his wife had been assaulted, and his dog had been killed? He asked the neighbor what had happened and the neighbor told him, 'Your agent came by. He raped your wife, killed your dog, and torched the house.' So the poor writer is in a state of shock, stumbling through the ashes of his house, and all he can say over and over again is 'My agent came by?'"

"Very funny," said Sylvia Lowell, without a hint

of mirth. "I think we're through for today, Mr. Snow."

"That wasn't exactly a ringing endorsement for my work."

"Speaking of ringing," she said, "my phone is ringing. Ciao, Walter."

She picked up the phone, began speaking to another client, and I got up and left with the usual bile rising in my throat, a feeling many authors experience after speaking with their agents. Oddly enough, as I left the building, I did not feel entirely discouraged. As Oscar Wilde, another writer who died broke, sick, misunderstood, drunk, unappreciated, and in the lonely rain of a Paris exile, said, "What fire doesn't destroy, it hardens." Sylvia Lowell had been wrong before. In fact, she'd been wrong many times before. If she'd been anything else besides an agent, they'd have shown her the door a long time ago.

I walked the ten blocks over to my editor's office and as I walked my resolve became stronger and my purpose in life became ever more lucid. For better or worse, I was a writer and write I must or my life was surely not sustainable. Love, happiness, satisfaction, peace of mind would all have to take a distant backseat to pushing little words around in various and sundry permutations whilst I prayed to what gods there existed above basement apartments to give me one good line and then to give me another. It was the only sure way to always keep Clyde and Fox close to me. It was the only way I could relate with the rest of the world. It was my chosen method of reminding myself that I was alive.

Steve Samet's office was small, cluttered with books and papers, and it did not give on to any view at all except an ugly, weatherbeaten brick wall. Steve wore a bow tie, an unfashionable, academic-style woolen jacket, and a perpetual cheerful disposition. In fact, he had what I often refer to as a terminal case of irritating Gentile optimism. All good editors are Gentiles; all good agents are Jewish. If you ever find yourself with a Jewish editor and a Gentile agent, you know you're in trouble. Steve also had three cats he liked to discuss incessantly with anyone who had the good grace to listen. Compared to Sylvia, Steve was a vertiable cheerleader for the cause. Exactly what the cause was, was an entirely different matter.

"Hey, big guy!" said Steve as I entered his office. "Love what you sent me. It's been a long time. Glad you're getting back on track."

"I never was off track," I said. "In fact, that was the problem. I was standing in the middle of the track and I got run over by a train."

"Love the new stuff," said Steve, as if I hadn't spoken at all. "When can I see some more?"

"Probably about the year 2010."

"Good. Keep it comin'. You really came up with some characters this time around. So vital. So alive. You've got a great imagination, Walter."

"Thanks, Steve."

"We've really got to try to get you on the Letterman show when this book comes out. I think Dave will really like you."

"I'd rather swallow my own vomit than be on that show."

"That's the spirit! What's the title of the book again?"

"*The Great Armenian Novel.*"

"Terrific title! The books'll be jumping off the shelves."

"They'll probably be jumping up people's asses."

"That, too," laughed Steve. "That, too!"

Steve was a real positive thinker. I figured him for a fairly early suicide but you never can tell. He was a company man and his agenda was to sell books for the publisher. It didn't matter to Steve whether the book was a posthumous collection of work by a poet who'd died in the gutter or a slick ghost written autobiography of Cher. He would champion the most vapid tissue of mainstream horseshit if it sold. If not, well, maybe David Letterman could help.

Steve gave me a hearty handshake and was now adjusting his bow tie, getting ready to go home to his cats. I didn't have any cats. I didn't even have a bow tie. All I had was a half-finished manuscript that my agent thought didn't work and my editor thought would jump off the shelves. Very possibly, I thought to myself as I left the building, they were both right.

Later that night, back at the apartment, I relived the two meetings in my mind. I was always somewhat disillusioned when I left Steve Samet's office. The one thing no author needs is an editor who loves his work, especially if it's for the wrong reason. Likewise, it's not the best thing in the world to have an agent who, essentially, dismisses you because you don't kill as many trees as Tom Clancy and whom you'd like to strangle every time you talk to her. When you boiled it all down, an author's only friends were himself and his words. Most authors didn't have much of a life. They couldn't be a Clyde or a Fox if they tried. They basically didn't know how to live. And it wasn't really them I was thinking about. It was me. All I could do was write. And when an author's personal life, pathetic as it may be, begins to spiral downward and disintegrate, it is invariably reflected on the page.

CHAPTER 22

In the dead of the night, I started to write. If Steve wanted more pages, I'd give him more pages. If Sylvia wanted more action, I'd give her more action. But first I felt it was necessary to write a true homage to Clyde and Fox. As characters, I had them down cold by now, I thought, and certainly I could complete the novel out of my own imagination, which is what every reader would believe it to be anyway. I did not need any longer to faithfully chronicle their ridiculous little hobbies and adventures out of the whole cloth of their existence. They were the characters and I was the author. I could now make them do or say anything I wanted. Maybe Clyde had been right all along. Maybe I *was* destroying them. What an odd occupation I had, I thought wryly. I was destroying them in order to create them. But it had to be done. And yet, I missed them. I realized, almost wistfully, that I might never see them again.

I started with Fox, hearing his voice in random past conversations, empathizing with his nuthouse background, getting inside his head. I felt like Faulkner, throwing the story to the winds. I felt like McMurtry, writing two hundred pages of boring shit before I really got going. I felt like solitary J.D. Salinger, who only mixed interpersonally to get inside the heads of real people and then cut them out of his life and nailed their hearts and souls to the page with a million typewriter keys. I felt like Fox and I felt crazy like a fox and I felt nothing. I said my farewells to Fox by writing a sort of stream-of-nervousness soliloquy in his voice and putting him back in a mental hospital:

A mental hospital is not always as romantic a place as it's cracked up to be. You always think of Ezra Pound or Vincent van Gogh or Zelda Fitzgerald or Emily Dickinson or Sylvia Plath or someone like that. Not that all the above-mentioned people resided in mental hospitals. All of them probably belonged there, but so do most people who don't reside in mental hospitals. I *know* Emily Dickinson never went into a mental hospital, but that's just because she never went anywhere except for brief walks in her garden with her dog, Austin. If she'd ever gone into a mental hospital and talked to the shrinks for a while, they never would have let her out. She might've done some good work there, but that would've been her zip code for the rest of her life. Now you take Van Gogh, for example. He lived in one with a cat and did some good work there. They put him in for wearing lighted candles on his hat while painting *The Night Cafe*. Today, the arbiters of true greatness, Japanese insurance companies, have determined that his work is worth millions. Sylvia Plath I don't know too much about except she wrote good prose and maybe some great poetry and then she put her head in an oven and killed herself, so by then it was too late to get her into a mental hospital. Everybody thought she was crazy for many years until her husband's second wife also croaked herself and then people began to wonder if maybe Sylvia had been all right and it was her fucking husband who was crazy. I mean, to have two wives conk on you like that, each one topping herself on your watch, pretty well indicated to most people outside mental hospitals that if that husband wasn't crazy, there was something wrong with him. Now Ezra Pound I don't know a hell of a lot about except he hated Jews and still managed to do some pretty good work in wig city. Hitler and Gandhi, both of whom belonged in wig city, for different reasons, no doubt, somehow managed to avoid the nuthouse circuit. They did, as we know, each spend a bit of time in prison, which in some ways is not as bad as being in a mental hospital except that you come out with an asshole the size of a walnut. In a sense, Hitler and Gandhi, who represent polar opposites of the human spirit, each found himself in prison where the absence of freedom and the distance from their dreams may have contributed to their achieving some pretty good work. Hitler, who hated Jews almost as much as Ezra Pound, wrote *Mein Kampf*, which was almost immediately translated into about fourteen languages and would have made him quite a favorite at literary cocktail parties if he'd been willing to stop there. Unfortunately, he couldn't hold a candle to Anne Frank. Gandhi, who spent his time in prison listening to a South African mob singing, "We're gonna hang ol' Gandhi from a green apple tree," did some scribbling of his own but mostly realized that he was tired of the London yuppie-lawyer drag and it was time for visions and revisions both sartorially as well as spiritually. But God only knows how Hitler and Gandhi, who were both interesting customers, would have fared had they been incarcerated in mental hospitals instead of prison. As it was, each man found himself creating and writing in the calaboose, something that almost never happens in a mental hospital because shrinks are constantly prescribing meds that keep you invariably, perpetually, hopelessly lost. Speaking of lost, Zelda Fitzgerald certainly qualifies in that category and technically, I suppose, she was confined to a "sanitarium," which was not truly a mental hospital if you want to be a purist about it but no doubt still probably had a sign in the lobby that read: "This Is Tuesday. The Next Meal Is Lunch." She'd been drinking a lot of her meals, evidently, and so they'd put her in this sanitarium in Asheville, North Carolina. The irony of the whole situation was that the sanitarium was in Asheville and the place burned down one night with Zelda and a fairly good-sized number of other no-hopers inside. I've wondered why God so often seems to send fires and other catastrophes to sanitariums and mental hospitals. It's kind of like swerving to hit a school bus. But all that being as it may, it's just ironic, I think, that the sanitarium burned down and that it was in Asheville. But before Zelda came along to screw things up, I was commenting on the fact that mental hospitals are far sadder and more sordid places than you'd think, as all these colorful, fragile, famous, ascetic people populate them. I mean, it isn't all Van Gogh and his cat. I mean, there are men following you with their penises shouting, "Am I being rude, Mother?" in frightening falsetto voices. People in mental hospitals shriek like mynah birds all the time. And masturbate. Dylan Thomas was a good one at that. He used to masturbate a lot but I don't think they ever put him in a mental hospital though God only knows he belonged there. And speaking of God only knows, Brian Wilson undoubtedly belongs there, too, except what would happen to the Beach Boys if you put Brian Wilson in the nuthouse? The only one of those guys who was really a surfer was Dennis Wilson. And you know what happened to him? He drowned! Ah well, the Channel swimmer always drowns in the bathtub, so they say. But I suppose I've come pretty far afield in this tawdry little tale that the shrinks would assuredly call a rambling discourse. If getting to the point is the determinant of whether or not you're crazy, then half the world's crazy. Trouble is, it's the wrong half. I mean, whoever said anything important by merely getting to the point? Did guys like Yeats and Shelley and Keats—who, by the way, all belonged in wig city—ever get to the point? I mean, what's the point of getting to the point? To show some shrink with a three-inch dick that you're stable, coherent, well-grounded? Wait—I haven't even gotten to Jesus yet. Sooner or later everybody in a mental hospital gets around to Jesus and it's a good thing that they do because I'll let you in on a little secret: Jesus doesn't talk to football coaches. He doesn't talk to televangelists or Bible Belt politicians or good little church workers or Christian athletes or anybody else in this God-fearing, godforsaken world. The only people Jesus ever really talks to are people in mental hospitals! They try to tell us but we never believe them. Why don't we, for Christ's sake? What have we got to lose? Millions of people in mental hospitals who say they've talked to Jesus can't all be wrong. It's the poor devils outside mental hospitals who are usually wrong or at least full of shit and that's probably why Jesus never talks to them. Anyway, you can probably tell by the fact that I'm not employing any paragraphs and the fact that this little rambling discourse tends to run on interminably that this looks like a mental-hospital letter itself. If that's what you think, you're right, because I am in a fucking mental hospital as I'm writing this tissue of horseshit and it's not one of those with green sloping lawns in that area between Germany and France that I always forget the name of. Hey, wait a minute! It's coming to me. Come baby come baby come baby come. Alsace-Lorraine! That's where the really soulful mental hospitals are. Unfortunately, I'm writing this from a mental hospital on the Mexican-Israeli border and I'm waiting for a major war to break out and they don't have any green sloping lawns. They don't even have any slopes. All they have is a lot of people who talk to Jesus, masturbate, and don't believe they belong in here. It's not a bad life, actually, once you get the hang of it, unless of course you hang yourself, which happens here occasionally, usually on a slow masturbation day. Anyway, the reason I'm telling you all this is because I don't really belong here. I've told the doctors. I've told the shrinks. I've even told a guy who thinks he's Napoleon. The guy's six feet tall, weighs two hundred and fifty pounds, and he's black, and he thinks he's Napoleon. I probably shouldn't have told him in the first place. The other day a woman reporter came in here from the local newspaper to do some kind of *Geraldo*-like exposé on the place and she interviewed some of the patients and one of them was me. I told her I was perfectly sane and I didn't belong in here. She asked me some questions and we chatted for a while and then she said that I sounded really lucid and normal to her and she agreed that I really didn't belong in here. Then she asked me, since I seemed so normal, what I was doing here in the first place and I told her I didn't know, that I just woke up one day and here I was and now the doctors won't let me out. She said for me not to worry. She said when she finished her exposé on my condition, these doctors would have to let me out. Then she shook my hand and headed for the door. About the time she put her hand on the doorknob. I took a Coke bottle and threw it real hard and hit her on the back of the head.

"Don't forget!" I shouted.

CHAPTER 23

Writing Fox's little diatribe from the mental hospital in what I imagined to be his own words and voice made me laugh and then made me start to feel lonely. I hated to admit it but I missed that visionary troublemaker more than I'd expected. And, if I permitted myself to think about it, I missed Clyde even more than I missed Fox. And most of all, I suppose, I missed that warm, alive feeling I usually had when the three of us were together. Writing about their exploits just wasn't quite the same as doing crazy things with them. What if the two of them had suddenly moved to another city or another country and I never saw either of them again in my life? Maybe Trump had pressed charges and made things hot for them. Maybe they'd just decided to let their Gypsy souls lead them out of town or even across the pond. I would, of course, be out ten thousand dollars on Fox's bail. But also, I thought, I would be out much, much more in the coin of the spirit, the money of childhood that can never truly be saved or counted. They would be free birds flying forever in someone else's sky, and I would be left to pick up the pieces of our star-crossed ephemeral friendship, trying to put it back together one little word at a time. It was a daunting, lonely task but it was a task I would not shirk. It was, I believed sadly and sincerely, what my life had come to. I now possessed what part of me had always wanted, I suppose: a writer's life. A romantic, monastic, lonely, mad, eviscerated, bloodless, empty, vicarious, melancholy, self-pitying, world-weary, futile, tormented, yet oddly glamorous writer's life. If I'd been writing a hundred years earlier, I'd probably have been working in a chilly garret in Paris or in a damp and windswept castle in Scotland. Anything to be cold.

It was very late, indeed, and I was thinking about Clyde. How I felt when she gave my hand a quick little squeeze. When she smiled that crooked, seductive smile that promised things I probably now would never receive. The way my life seemed to always brighten when she called me Sunshine.

Books get dusty. Paper is such a lonely thing. Paper is so sad before you fill it with ridiculous little words. It makes you feel like Dr. Zhivago after losing Lara, gazing out over an endless, aching, snowy plain of nothing but sorrow and empty and white. There is nothing to replace a lover, nothing to replace a friend. But that is where you have to start if you want to be a writer or an artist or a man.

I thought of the words of Robert Louis Stevenson: "It is a better thing by far that the lad should break his neck, than that you should break his spirit." Was it actually in the realm of conceivability that I could cause harm to the spirits of my maybe erstwhile, maybe forever friends merely by capturing their odd little hobbies and their great hopeless dreams and thoughts in a web of words? Clyde could not have been right about that, could she? She was somewhere out there in the rest of the world and I was here alone in the basement with only cigarettes and coffee, a little lamp, and a growing pile of numbered pages for companions on a journey of bleakness and despair. Could the mere mechanics of writing, chronicling, articulating an abstract notion such as love or life or friendship make that very entity go away? Wasn't writing just another occupation like any other, only more futile and perverse? Did Clyde truly have some Gypsy background similar to the American Indian that ingrained in her being, like a flashing railroad crossing sign, not to let anyone take a photograph of you for fear it would surely suck away another small piece of your soul and keep you from becoming an Indian when you grew up?

I was thinking about Clyde. I was writing about Clyde. I was just getting ready to light a cigarette. That's what I was doing when the buzzer sounded for the front door. It startled me slightly. Except for Clyde and Fox, I was not in the habit of receiving visitors in the middle of the night. I walked warily over to the intercom, pushed the button, and said, "Who's there?" It was not a very original thing to say but at that hour of the night I was fresh out of creativity. What creativity I'd had was undoubtedly lying somewhere on a snowy plain in Russia. A voice came back to me through the intercom. It was a warm, familiar, feminine voice. It said, "Let me in or I'll blow your house down." I buzzed the front door open immediately and opened the door to my apartment and in walked Clyde, fragrant and cool as a sailor's dream.

"You've done a lot with this place," she said facetiously, looking around the barren flat. Her eyes at last settled on the typewriter and the stack of pages. "You've done a lot," she said again, softer this time.

Impulsively, she walked around the desk, picked up a page, and casually perused the manuscript. She put it down and picked up another. In the lamplight, her countenance was that of a porcelain poker face and she looked as beautiful as I'd ever seen her. I'd never been very objective, of course, when it came to Clyde. I stood there watching her quietly as she read two or three more pages and put them back on the desk. Then she stared out the window into the darkness and her face seemed to soften, making her slightly less imperial and, if possible, even more attractive.

"Not bad," she said at last. "I like the 'crooked seductive smile.'"

"I do, too," I said. "It's very seductive. Not to mention crooked."

"It's comforting to know the book is good."

"Did you ever doubt it?"

"Not really, Walter. It might just be kind of fun to be a literary heroine. And speaking of heroin, don't believe all that gibberish Fox is feeding you about my being a heroin addict. Fox was the heroin addict. I didn't even know him then but he's mentioned it to me many times. He's just trying to stir up a little trouble between us. He is a world-class troublemaker, you know."

"I do know. Were you really in a carnival?"

"The carnival was allegorical. Just about everything in my life is allegorical, now that I think about it. With me, you've got to read between the lines, or, in your case, write between the lines. Whatever you want me to be, you'll probably discover that I am."

"What if I want to make an honest woman out of you?" I said.

"What if I just want to suck your cock?" she replied.

She looked through me then and her eyes flashed like tilt lights on a pinball machine. There was no smile on her lips, crooked, seductive, or otherwise. She was being serious. Even more frightening, she seemed to mean what she said. I held my breath. For that defining moment, all of New York City appeared to have come under a storybook spell. All traffic and sound and belief were suddenly suspended in a vacuum of something close to childlike awe. Then our eyes met, our bodies standing as motionless as statues in a park. When she spoke again, it was in a husky whisper.

"Well," she said, "do we have any takers?"

Somewhere in the night, a statue in the park raised his hand and it was me. That was all Clyde needed. She came around the desk like a madwoman. Soon I was on the floor, my pants were off, and her head was between my thighs devouring my manhood like some carnivorous creature on the African veldt. Occasionally, I could catch the flash of her eyes as her hands tightened around my legs and her head began to bob robotically. She probably would have sent my penis to Venus quite rapidly if I hadn't noticed, on a downward bob cycle, that a figure was standing at the window.

Lying on my back, I was able to get up on my elbows high enough to obtain an unimpeded view on the following down cycle. Incredible as it seemed, Fox was standing outside the window wearing some kind of night-vision goggles over his eyes. Normally, this would have been enough to have made anybody's pasta at least slightly al dente, but Clyde was doing something different now and it seemed to be keeping everyone in the game. I became suddenly aware that she had taken both of my balls in her mouth and was making achingly slow, ruthless circles with her head, first going in one direction for a few passes, then reversing and going in the other. I laid my head back on the floor and closed my eyes.

Then several things happened at once. My body started to tremble and I knew it would be only a matter of moments before the hostages would be released, yet, at the same time, I could hear an incessant buzzing noise in my head. I couldn't tell at first from what point the noise was coming. All I knew for sure was that I was coming. I thought that the sexual act had been so powerful that an auditory hallucination had accompanied the climax. Then I heard a disembodied voice that I gradually realized was emanating from the intercom.

"Walter, are you there?" it said. "Open up! It's me. Clyde."

Like a man in a dream I walked over to the intercom, buzzed her in to the building, and opened my door. Moments later, Clyde came in and appeared to be looking at me rather strangely.

"You seem out of breath, Walter," she said. "Are you all right?"

"I'm fine," I said. "In fact, I was just—um—-thinking about you."

"Only *thinking* about me?"

"Yes, of course," I said, recovering quickly. "I haven't seen you for a while and I've missed you."

"Let's go for a walk," she said.

"A walk? It's almost two o'clock in the morning."

"What else have you got to do?" she said.

We walked in silence for a while, taking in the

nocturnal sights of the city. There were more people on the streets than you would have thought at that hour, stragglers, hell-raisers, lost boys and girls, denizens of the night. At one point, Clyde took my hand and gave it a little squeeze and things were almost all right for a time. Then I started feeling like a man in a dream again. I nearly found myself wondering if I was a man walking with a woman down a street in the night or if all this was merely taking place within the confines of my novel. And as we walked, questions popped into my mind unbidden. Was it possible for a bad man to write a good book? Could a cold, jaded, selfish man, increasingly incapable of emitting even a spark of human warmth, push little words around in such a fraudulent fashion as to fool the world into believing he'd written a decent, serviceable, even compelling novel? The answer to both of those questions I now clearly realized was yes.

And now another question came into my mind, the answer of which I was only vaguely aware: Was I rapidly, hopelessly, inexorably turning into that man?

We came upon the familiar corner where the bar known as the Unicorn had once stood. The sign was gone now, but in its place was another. It read: "Coming Soon. Grand Opening. Starbucks."

There must have still been hope for me because I could feel Clyde's heart explode as she stood beside me. Even had we known it was coming,

I thought, there was nothing we could have done about it. Like it or not, it was a sign of the times. But, as we would soon discover, it would prove to be much more than that. It would mean more than societal evolution or corporate greed. It would come to represent the crowning glory of the bond of our little triumvirate, the spiritual high-water mark of that reckless, fragile entity that was Clyde and Fox and myself. Like a noxious vapor, its proud and bland confidence would come to embody the very destruction of us all.

CHAPTER 24

Nothing ever really changes, I suppose, in New York or anywhere else in this tedious, unpleasant, never-ending, non-fiction world. Fundamental change is virtually impossible for our species. Like little chirpies, we build our nests and construct our buildings, which time and terrorists and termites try to tear down. Like leaf-cutter ants, we construct our highways that connect many different places in such a way that eventually they all become so similar there's no point in going anywhere to begin with. Like beavers, we build our bridges so when things aren't going very well people can jump off and kill themselves, which is probably what I should have done the first time Clyde and I saw that Starbucks sign. But, of course, I didn't. I wanted to live. I wanted to paint. I wanted to complete my great Armenian novel. And, to be sure, eventually I did. But completing my literary opus did not bring fundamental changes to my life. Far from it. What it brought, or wrought, I should say, was a series of rather meaningless, superficial changes that everybody, including myself, thought at the time were important. They weren't, of course. They never are.

I don't, by the way, believe the compilation of the novel had a thing to do with the disastrous events that occurred in the lives of Clyde and Fox. Writing a novel is just what is sounds like—writing a novel. It doesn't harm children or green plants or chirpies. It's just putting someone you love between two covers without remembering to kiss them good night. Then you leave them there forever as you move on to your next project. But it can't be too lonely when you're sandwiched between two covers. People usually look in from time to time.

But let me redirect the conversation back to myself again for a moment. I was as much to blame as anybody for what occurred at Starbucks. What started out perhaps as one of our little hobbies moved quickly to a full-blooded passion, and then, in the end, to an unstoppable, unsinkable, unholy crusade.

It had not been precisely clear from the Starbucks sign exactly when the grand opening was to take place. Clyde had suggested that it was a good opportunity for me to do some "legwork." As always with Clyde, I acquiesced. It would not be difficult, she had suggested, especially since I lived in the neighborhood, for me to "sniff around a little bit." Then, she averred, we would bring in the "big guns." The big guns, I was given to understand, were Fox and herself. Though I was mildly piqued by this characterization of my abilities relative to hers and Fox's, I did not at the time let it show. There have been many times in my life when I have not let my true feelings show and I have seldom regretted it. Indeed, there is little in my life that I have truly come to regret, always excepting, of course, the loss of Clyde.

So getting back to that night we saw the Starbucks sign hanging on the old Unicorn, I guess I could say that that was the road-to-Damascus experience that led circumstances to be as they are today.

I did Clyde's bidding the following afternoon and it didn't take long for me to talk to a few workmen on the building and ascertain where things stood with the Grand Opening. As soon as I had the information, I called Clyde.

"The grand opening is this coming Monday," I told her.

"Good," she said. "We've got the whole week-end to get ready."

"To get ready for what?"

"For the grand opening, of course. You didn't think we were going to take this lying down, did you?"

"Well, no, but—"

"This is *war!* This is the first real chance you'll get to see Fox don his sword and shield!"

"I've seen him don his stethoscope."

"You haven't seen anything yet. This is going to be an extended, strategic, pitched battle of almost military precision. You are about to witness a battlefield genius on the level of Robert E. Lee at work!"

I started to say "Save your Confederate money," but I thought better of it. One of the many charming attributes that had accrued to the persons of Fox and Clyde over the years was their almost total disregard for whether or not they ever won or lost in any of their endeavors. Winning was never really important to them. What was important, Fox had once told me, was the way you selected your enemies. Donald Trump was a worthy opponent, he'd thought. So was taking on Bellevue Hospital. To tackle a big and powerful enemy, he'd said, was a mark of humanity and courage. Fox liked Rosa Parks because she'd single-handedly taken on the institution of segregation. He'd admired Natan Sharansky for going up against the entire Soviet Union. And he'd especially appreciated Don Quixote for taking on all the combined forces of evil in the world. "Who a man's enemies are," Fox had said, "tells you more about the man than his friends." So I did not point out to Clyde that Robert E. Lee's team had lost the Civil War. In fact, I did not point out anything because she was already giving me my marching orders.

"We'll all reconnoiter at the command post tomorrow afternoon at fourteen hundred," she said.

"That's a good plan," I said. "Where's the command post?"

"It's a place that'll be very convenient for you,

Walter. It's your apartment. It's not only strategically located near Starbucks, it's also not readily visible from the street."

"It's also a basement apartment," I pointed out, "which could come in handy in case Starbucks decides to resort to nuclear weapons."

"It's perfect," said Clyde, ignoring my facetious tone. "See you there tomorrow at fourteen hundred, soldier."

"Yes, sir," I said sharply.

Well, here we were again, I said to myself as I hung up the phone. We'd gotten away, or almost gotten away with, all our little hobbies thus far, and there were a number that, for various reasons, I've chosen not to include in this manuscript. I've left them out, in all honesty, either because they made me look bad or for fear of possibly becoming criminally liable for them in some way. As an author of quasi-legendary fiction you may choose whether or not you wish to protect the innocent. But there are several other matters that assume a more paramount importance. One: You must protect yourself at all costs. Two: If you must harm the innocent, make sure you don't harm the flow. For that, no one will ever forgive you.

I was quite frankly of two minds regarding whatever plans Fox and Clyde had cooked up for Starbucks. Part of me realized that, if I chronicled events faithfully just as they actually happened, it would undoubtedly make great fiction. But I also realized, of course, that crossing swords with this monolithic megamonster could be extremely dangerous to one's health. This hardly daunted my compatriots, however. They wanted blood. They wanted justice for the underdog. They wanted, above and beyond everything else, to have a good time. I must confess, in my heart of hearts, that I did not truly share their dreams, ideals, or desires. I wasn't afraid of blood, and justice was okay, too, and I didn't mind having a good time. But most of all, I wanted good material. It wasn't long in coming.

At fourteen hundred sharp on the following afternoon, I watched as Fox and Clyde invaded my humble abode. They came in full regalia and bearing enough luggage to stay for a month. Clyde looked very appetizing in a short leather skirt and black pumps and carrying her ubiquitous briefcase. Fox wore a military-looking khaki suit with a MacArthur-like field commander's cap and a long white silk scarf.

"All you're missing," I commented dryly, "are the Snoopy goggles."

"They're probably in his suitcase," said Clyde.

"This trunk," said Fox, for it was more of a steamer trunk than a suitcase, "contains practically everything we need to make Starbucks wish they'd never been born."

"Well, for God's sake," I said, growing a bit curious in spite of myself, "open it up."

"I said *practically* everything we need," said Fox. "First we need to sit down and have a little talk and make sure that we're all on the same page."

"He's not referring to the manuscript," said Clyde coyly.

"Fine," I said. "I'll make some coffee. *Not* the Starbucks variety, of course."

"Good," said Fox. "Got a smoke?"

"Sure, pal," I said, giving Fox a cigarette and taking one for myself, "but I thought you'd prefer the one-hitter."

"Not now," said Fox, waving the notion off as I lit his cigarette and then my own. "If I'm going to direct this campaign, I've got to keep my mind totally clear. Well, at least as clear as it ever gets. Let's start things off with a question for both of you. From whence does the name 'Starbucks' derive?"

"I've got no idea," I said, putting on the non-Starbucks coffee.

"Is this trivia quiz really necessary?" asked Clyde, reclining on the small sofa and stretching her body in a highly sensuous manner.

"Damn straight," said Fox. "We're getting to know our enemy. Walter, as a literary man, I'm surprised that you don't know the answer."

"There's a lot of things I don't know," I said, "and one of them is how to start this coffeemaker."

"Let me do it," said Clyde. "Fox is the trouble-maker. I'll be the homemaker."

"That'll be the day," said Fox. "Anyway, com-rades, the name 'Starbucks' comes from the nice

223

first mate, Mr. Starbuck, in Melville's great epic, *Moby-Dick*. He pleaded with Captain Ahab to let Moby-Dick go, but Ahab was obsessed with the great white whale and wouldn't hear of it."

"What does this have to do with our latest little hobby?" asked Clyde, not unreasonably.

"Patience, my dear friends," said Fox. "As they say in the East, 'Slowly, slowly catchee monkey.'"

At this point, I went over to my little notebook and, as unobtrusively as possible, jotted down Fox's colorful phrase. Fox fairly beamed with gratification upon witnessing my small effort. Clyde, on the other hand, sent a dark scowl in my direction. Impassively, I placed the pen and pad back down on the desk. Fox continued his lecture.

"Melville, as you probably know, Walter, already had two huge mainstream successes under his belt before he wrote *Moby-Dick*. But *Typee* and *Omoo* were merely highly popular potboilers. They only reflected the culture; they didn't subvert it. But he put his heart and mind and soul into *Moby-Dick*, and when it came out, it tanked so bad that you could only find it in the whaling section of bookstores. Melville spent the rest of his life languishing in almost total obscurity as custom inspector number seventy-five. When he died, the *New York Times* misspelled his name in the obit. 'The important books,' said Herman Melville, 'are the books that fail.' Today, of course, we recognize *Moby-Dick* as one of the greatest works in Western literature."

"Where do I go to drop this course, Professor?" said Clyde laconically.

"You don't go anywhere," said Fox. "The course is required."

"The only thing that's required," said Clyde with some heat, "is that you open that fucking trunk right now!"

"Children, please!" I said. "How can we hope to succeed against Starbucks if we're fighting amongst ourselves?"

"Walter's right," said Clyde. "Now open the fucking trunk."

Fox, displaying as much dignity as he could under the circumstances, moved smoothly from the Melville lecture to the nuts and bolts of the battle plan itself. He fumbled briefly with the combination lock, then grandly flung the lid open on the steamer trunk. As if the contents of the trunk itself possessed some strange, mystical power, Fox's very demeanor seemed to be transformed, from that of the philosopher to that of the general. His manner was suddenly clipped, confident, and, oddly, almost inspirational. Like a man possessed, he began removing various and sundry items and what appeared to be a pharmacopoeia of potions from the trunk and placing them on the desk. Clyde and I watched in fascinated silence. At last, gesturing toward the desk, Fox spoke.

"This," he said, "is Operation Diarrhea."

This strange pronouncement was greeted by a silence in the small room. It did not seem, however, to deter Fox's forward progress in any significant manner. I glanced at Clyde but she appeared to be gazing at Fox with an expression that bordered upon rapture.

"Amazing," I said. "You're the only person I know who, in the space of five minutes, can move facilely from Herman Melville to Operation Diarrhea."

"I told you he was a genius," said Clyde simply.

I nodded in agreement because I totally agreed. Fox was crazy as a bedbug but he was also clearly and undeniably a genius. Incredible as it seems to me now, I was ready to follow him into battle. I was also, of course, ready to follow Clyde. Anywhere.

"I'll go over it slowly," Fox was saying, "in case anyone has any questions. The first thing we do is deactivate the dumper. Then we work from the toilet out. I will put the one unisexual toilet out of commission on Monday just before the place closes. I'll flush these two sponges, which will be wet and curled in a tube, and they'll expand in the pipe. Just for fun, I'll Saran-Wrap the toilet itself so the first diarrhea victim will really get a nasty surprise. Question, Walter?"

"Yes. You have quite a little apothecary there. How can you be sure all these potions will have the desired effect and how can you be sure nobody will get seriously hurt by ingesting them?"

"Good questions, Walter, good questions. No combinations of these products will cause serious long-term illness but any of the three will cause immediate and extremely unpleasant reactions. Clyde will place them in the appropriate sugars and creamers and syrups at the same time I'm working on the toilet. Now, Clyde, this is powder of the senna plant, which produces severe abdominal cramps. It goes in the sugar containers. And this is called cascara sagrada, an additive from the dried root of the Arizona and New Mexico thorny cactus. I got it in pure form right from the health food store. Taken in any form, it causes almost instant diarrhea, which is where this little project gets its name, Operation Diarrhea."

"An attractive name," said Clyde.

"Not as attractive as Starbucks is going to be once it goes into effect. Now the third product is the very potent syrup of ipecac, which, of course, goes into their syrups, and which, of course, causes what is known in the trade as severe projectile vomiting. Now, I'll be disabling the toilet, Clyde will plant the three additives, and Walter will be doing what he's already demonstrated he has a unique talent for, distracting the brewmasters or whatever the hell they call themselves. No offense, Walter, but of the three of us, you look the most like a normal Starbucks customer. So you'll talk to the people behind the counter about your recent coffee-tasting trip to Sumatra or something while I do the toilet and Clyde does the condiments. Then Tuesday morning, the day after the grand opening, all hell should break loose. The only customers who will survive Operation Diarrhea will be the ones who take their coffee black or those who use half-and-half in those little plastic containers.

"In a typical New York clientele there's bound to be a sizable handful of lawyers who will sue the shit—this time quite literally—out of Starbucks. This might not break their business operation, but it'll certainly give them pause. It'll also be fun to watch."

"So you don't think Operation Diarrhea will be enough to get them to close the store?" asked Clyde.

"Doubtful," said Fox. "But it's only our first shot over the bow. This is a war, and Operation Diarrhea is only the first battle. It doesn't matter what you do in war or life just as long as you win the last battle or learn the last and greatest lesson. If Operation Diarrhea isn't enough, we move on to Operation Elephant Dump Numbers One, Two, and Three. Then there's always La Cucaracha. You know what that means in Spanish?"

Neither Clyde nor I knew what it meant. We waited for the great general to enlighten us.

"It means 'cockroach,'" said Fox.

"Let's hope it doesn't come to that," said Clyde. "I *hate* cockroaches."

"So will Starbucks," said Fox. "But first things first."

Without further ado, he took a large flat object out of his magician's trunk and, as Clyde and I watched in silence, he unfolded a large collapsible bulletin board of the variety you might find in the Pentagon and began searching for a convenient wall upon which to hang it. With the help of Clyde and myself, the bulletin board was finally hung on the far wall, complete with multicolored flags and thumbtacks so it looked very official and military.

"This will be our flowchart," said Fox. "No pun intended. If the store closes, of course, we take it down and everybody goes home happy. But remember, as our campaign continues, it will become more and more difficult to carry on operations inside the store. If they don't have video cameras now, they'll put them up. Also, they'll put security in place and they'll know what we look like and they'll be watching for us. We may have to alter our appearances rather drastically and even that may prove risky. And don't forget, the Starbucks organization, or the Starbucks family, as they like to call it, has very deep pockets. We must fight like guerrillas. Like Jesse James and Robin Hood and Che Guevara and Ho Chi Minh. This is a campaign of attrition, of disruption, of harassment. Don't expect our first foray to be the knockout punch. But if we are persistent, clever, and courageous, we will prevail. And believe me, comrades, we will definitely get their attention with Operation Diarrhea."

I looked at the bulletin board, then over to Fox, and then I glanced at Clyde for her reaction, but she had gotten up and walked over to the kitchen. A moment later, she returned bearing a small tray.

"Coffee, anyone?" she said.

CHAPTER 25

I'm not ashamed to report that during the remainder of that weekend I felt more than I ever had in my life like a kid waiting for Christmas. There was a new chemistry that sang in my soul, a new entity being born every time the three of us put our combined hearts and minds in a deliciously dangerous new little project. And if, as Fox alleged, the size of your enemies had anything to do with your spiritual stature, we were verging on becoming secular saints. You could look for a long time and never find a bigger, more insidious opponent than Starbucks. How could three little people in this crazy world ever hope to even dent the armor of one of the greatest of all modern one-eyed giants? We would soon see.

I had to admit that there was definitely something exhilarating, maybe even magical, that occurred inside me whenever Clyde and Fox became actively engaged in my life. It was surely the only time I truly felt alive. And, as a mildly disconcerting side effect, I had begun to see and think of the two of them almost as one person. Clyde and Fox were like one human force with the undeniable ability to stir my cautious, weary, weather-beaten soul. Yet I realized, unlike them, that what we were doing was wrong. Well, "wrong" is not quite the right word. The things we did were not really wrong, only perhaps in the narrowest legal sense. "Wrong" is again the wrong word. I take it back. The events we became involved in were not wrong. Futile, certainly. Possibly star-crossed and highly addictive. The time we shared was like walking out on a precarious limb of humanity with the net consisting of only our little group of three.

As crazy as it sounds, I found myself looking forward to Monday night at ten o'clock, for ten o'clock, we had learned, was to be the daily closing time for this particular Starbucks store. Not that there is a great deal of difference between one Starbucks and another, which is part of the insidious poison that is inherent in any large chain establishment today. One may believe that "something different" might be the spice of life and might have an innate appeal to basic human nature, but nothing could be further from the truth. People are invariably more like me than they are like Clyde or Fox. We live in a world, I'm afraid, of cautious, careful, conservative little Walter Snows. Fox was not wrong in his assessment: I *do* look like the typical Starbucks customer. I probably even feel and think like the typical Starbucks customer. The only two differences are that I hate myself for it and I write down all my self-loathing.

Monday morning broke cold and clear over New

York City. How ridiculous, I thought as I woke up, to feel excited, even vaguely privileged, to be involved in something as crude, crass, and meaningless as Operation Diarrhea. No good could come of it, I felt. And yet I felt strangely drawn to this unlikely, even unpleasant affair by forces beyond my control. It was almost like a heroin addict must feel when he (or she) places a bit more of the product on the spoon each time, gambling on just how much he might take without killing himself. The seeds had already been sown. Now the harvest, for better or worse, for good or evil, must be reaped.

Clyde had called late in the afternoon to see how I was doing and to ask if I had any qualms about the "new project."

"I just feel a little uneasy about using all those chemicals," I'd said. "You know how it is when pranksters sometimes slip various drugs into the punch bowl? It's not supposed to happen, of course, but every now and then somebody dies."

"Dear sweet little Sunshine," she'd said. I brightened considerably in spite of myself. "No one's going to get seriously hurt by consuming these chemicals. They might *wish* they could die, but that's all."

"You're sure of that?" I'd asked again.

"But of course, darling," she'd said breezily. "The only people who stand any chance of getting killed are the three of us."

I always felt better after talking with Clyde, and

that conversation definitely made me feel better. I was still feeling pretty good at nine-fifteen that evening when the three of us headed out from my apartment for the short, two-block trek to Starbucks. Clyde looked fetching, I thought, in a pair of men's khaki slacks, a black knit top that fit her very snugly, and a khaki photographer's vest with lots of pockets everywhere to conceal many small vials of senna plant, cascara sagrada, and syrup of ipecac. Fox wore a trench coat concealing the now-wet sponges rubber-banded tightly together in a tubelike configuration small enough to comfortably go down the toilet before expanding in the pipe. The sponges were wrapped in Saran Wrap, which would double for a toilet bowl cover. "The rubber bands come off," Fox confided in us, "before the sponges go down."

"That's a handy thing to know," I said, adjusting my Yankees cap and the sweater that Clyde had tied around my neck. With a pair of faux horn-rimmed glasses and a bright red tie slightly askew, I looked perfect, according to Clyde, for the part.

"You look like the yuppie who came in from the cold," said Clyde admiringly.

"Are you sure it's not typecasting?" said Fox.

"All I'm sure of," I said, "is that if I don't come in from the cold soon, I'm going to freeze my ass off."

"Just be sure you take your coffee black," said Clyde, giving me a playful goose in the ass. It was a surprisingly intimate gesture and I will admit that it set my heart racing slightly. I waited to see if Fox would react in any way but he did not. He was totally focused, apparently, on Operation Diarrhea.

We walked about a block in silent contemplation. It felt as if we were three troublemakers in some kind of crazy spaghetti Western. Moving in for the showdown. Moving in for the kill. It felt good. It felt more than good. It felt like Walter Snow was finally, vibrantly alive and a part of something special. Then, with about a block still to go, Clyde suddenly stopped and grabbed Fox by the trench coat.

"Wait a minute," she said. "There's something I'm not sure of."

"Don't get cold feet now," said Fox. "It's nine-thirty and counting."

"I just want to go over something," she said. "You'll be safely in the bathroom deactivating the toilet and Walter here will be harmlessly chatting up the brewmasters or whatever the hell they call themselves behind the counter. But I'm the one whose movements could look very suspicious. I'm the one the salespeople or the cameras actually could catch."

"That's a very good point," said Fox, "and I'm glad you brought it up. I'll go in first and if there are cameras, I'll come right back out and we'll begin preparations immediately for Operation Cockroach Bomb and Operation Elephant Dump Numbers One, Two, and Three."

"That's fine," said Clyde, "but what if the brewmasters catch me red-handed? What if they nail my ass?"

"No offense, Clyde," said Fox, "but it's a pretty nice ass. As Teddy would say, 'You got some junk in the trunk!'"

"Hey," I said. "What about Teddy? He'd be a perfect man to have on our side in this campaign."

"C'mon, give me some credit," said Fox. "I've already thought of Teddy. But I'm not bringing him in until after Operation Cockroach Bomb."

"I'll probably be watching that one from the calaboose," said Clyde.

"No, you won't," said Fox. "Let me give you a few little helpful tips. When you first go in, put in a big order for your whole bridge club or something. Twelve latte frappachuchis. Something like that."

"And I'll be sure and get a receipt so I can sue the shit out of them as well."

"Isn't she a sweet kid?" said Fox, getting misty-eyed. "She doesn't miss a step. Okay, now while they're making your order, it's natural for you to be browsing in the place and looking at stuff. Keep the vials in the palm of your hand, sort of a sleight-of-hand job. Hey, Walter. Has Clyde ever given you her famous sleight-of-hand job?"

"He wishes," said Clyde, who was so on the money that I almost blushed. She capped it off with a wicked, telling wink in my direction.

"And here's the perfect way to justify your

behavior if you happen to catch one of them looking at you with a suspicious eye. Just pretend the sugar bowl or cream container is stuck and you're having a little trouble opening it. They see that. Then they see you get it open. Then they don't look at you anymore."

"That's what I wanted to hear," said Clyde with renewed confidence. "Fox knows everything, doesn't he, Walter?"

"Just about," I said.

"Remember the Unicorn!" shouted Fox, moving on toward our little date with destiny. "All those for freedom, follow me! Our only enemies are time and Starbucks and there may not be an army in the world that can defeat them but if three crazy Americans can't do it I'll let you lay your dick on my wisdom tooth!"

"Quite a battle cry," I remarked to Clyde, with Fox ten steps ahead of us and out of earshot. "Tell me, is he gay?"

"Terms like that don't apply to Fox," she said. "He likes all flavors. If more people were as crazy, as thoughtful, and as unconventional as Fox, it would be a better world."

"Amen to that," I said, but I don't know that Clyde heard me. Clyde and Fox were ahead of me now, moving toward Starbucks like heat-seeking missiles. I had to move quickly to catch up with them. And I found that I wanted to catch up with them. Whatever insane, inane antics they were involved in at any given moment, I wanted to be a part of them, of whatever they had, of whatever they were.

"This is a wonderful, medium-bodied coffee," I found myself saying to the barista only a matter of moments later. That's what they called themselves. Baristas. Not brewmasters. At Starbucks, I was to quickly find, they have another name for everything and no matter what you call something, they will invariably correct you, politely, if rather patronizingly.

"Actually, it's one of our *light-bodied* blends," said the barista as she readjusted a ring in her left eyebrow.

"This *is* Sumatran, right?" I ventured. Out of the corner of my eye, I could see Clyde moving about the store, poking into things.

"Sumatran *blend*," said the barista, checking her watch. It was getting close to the ten o'clock closing time and she looked more than ready to start shutting things down.

"It does appear to have a rather bold acidity," I said. "A friend of mine once worked with the Peace Corps in Kalimantan, Indonesia. I think he was an agricultural extension worker or something. His job was to distribute seeds downriver to the natives but the Peace Corps failed to send him any seeds. Eventually, he was forced to distribute his own seed downriver, which led to some rather unpleasant repercussions—"

"Excuse me! Excuse me, miss!" came a strident, mildly irritated female voice from the far end of the counter. "Can I have twelve frappuccinos to go, please? It's Little Italy night at our condo."

"Everything is prepared to go," the barista pointed out. "Twelve frappuccinos!" she said to a black man who seemed to have materialized from a cubbyhole somewhere and who very much resembled a young Lionel Ritchie.

"And I'd like a receipt, please," said Clyde. "I'll have to present it for reimbursement at the meeting."

There were a few other people making last-minute purchases, I noticed, and this screened Clyde even further from the eyes of the people behind the counter. Another positive note was that the lids and container tops seemed to be large enough to help shield the small vials with which she was industriously working. On the downside, the place was really beginning to thin out. It was almost ten.

"I'll have a double espresso, please," came a suave male voice just over my right shoulder.

"That's a *doppio*," said the barista to the man.

"And may I also have a key to the rest room?"

The woman with the eyebrow ring screamed "One *doppio!*" at Lionel Ritchie and then handed the man behind me a rest-room key that appeared to be attached to a large red Easter basket of some sort. I dared not look around as Fox's trench-coated arm reached right in front of me to retrieve the key. "Pardon my boardinghouse reach," he said, chuckling politely to himself. Fox

239

was cutting it very close, timewise, but there was really no decent way the key could be denied him. He would, it appeared, definitely be the last customer to use the rest room. After him, I thought with a smile, it might not be used for a longer time than Starbucks expected. At least not very successfully.

"So my friend asked the Peace Corps to send him some coffee beans," I continued, in an effort to distract the people behind the counter who now numbered three, but they all appeared so busy with tallying things, preparing a dozen frappuccinos, and closing up shop that my monologue was almost unnecessary. Clyde was putting a few finishing touches on some sugar bowls and she didn't seem to be drawing any attention. My monologue didn't seem to be drawing much attention either, but I didn't let it hurt my feelings or slow me down. I wanted to do my part.

"By the time the coffee beans finally arrived," I droned on relentlessly, "some sort of tribal dispute had occurred in the region. I recall my friend telling me how he drove the load of coffee beans down the highway, running over hundreds of arrows in his Land Rover. Well, it wasn't really *his* Land Rover. There was a wealthy plantation owner who lived nearby and he had a beautiful blond daughter. I think it was her father's Land Rover. My friend always had quite a way with the women. By the time the daughter took the Land Rover back to her father, there was a spear sticking out of the front grillwork. Unfortunately, there was also a spear sticking out of my friend's penis."

It didn't really matter what I said. None of the Starbucks people were listening. They were in the seriously elaborate process of closing up and trying politely to urge me to leave. Clyde had paid for her frappuccinos and was collecting her all-important receipt for her meeting at the condo that didn't exist, just, of course, as my friend with the coffee beans didn't exist. I let Clyde leave first. Then I took my departure, which must have been a great relief to the people who were exploring the possibilities of advancement in their Starbucks careers.

I met up with Clyde about a block away and we loitered on the corner congratulating ourselves. No doubt we both looked somewhat flushed, pardon the expression, from the excitement of the apparent success of the operation.

"Now where the hell is Fox?" I asked. "This waiting for him is starting to make me nervous.'"

"Don't worry, Sunshine," said Clyde sweetly. "Fox always comes through. In the meantime, there's something I've always wanted to say to you."

"What, darling?"

"Care for a frappuccino?"

CHAPTER 26

Bright and early the next morning, Fox and Clyde woke me up like Huck Finn, throwing stones against my basement apartment window as if I were an urban-dwelling Tom Sawyer. Or was it Tom Sawyer who threw stones against Huck Finn's window? It really doesn't matter, I suppose. As an author, or literary man, as Fox would have it, it's possible that I've faulted myself unfairly for not being certain of these things. Fox's little lecture on Herman Melville was still mildly rankling as well, conceivably because I'd learned things about Melville I'd never known. Of course, nobody really knew much about Melville. That was the glory of being an author: successfully creating something that would outlive your own bones. Like a great white whale, a maniacal ship captain, and a first mate someone would someday name a chain of corporate coffee shops after. For all I knew, Huck Finn might have been throwing stones at Melville's window. Anyway, Fox and Clyde awakened me in this prepubescent fashion and I woke up and realized it was six-thirty in the morning. I staggered over to the door and buzzed them in.

They seemed to hurl themselves into the room like a pair of human harpoons, both in an arc of constant kinetic energy. They paced back and forth excitedly as I struggled to get dressed, brush my teeth, and comb my hair. Indeed, the two of them seemed so full of life it almost felt as if I were a single adult looking after two small children.

"Hurry up," said Fox. "They're probably starting without us."

"It's going to be great!" shouted Clyde. "If it works."

"Of course it'll work! I'll bet it's already started!"

"Hurry up, Walter! We could be missing the greatest show on earth!"

"Will you two please control yourselves!" I mumbled in exasperation. "I'm trying to brush my teeth!"

About five minutes later, the three of us, bundled up against the chill, damp morning, headed out the door and down the street toward Starbucks to pay witness to the fruits of our nefarious labors. At this hour of the morning, the Village looked almost beautiful, waking up against the dawn with most of the stores still shuttered and most of the people still sleeping. We stopped at a little bakery, got doughnuts and coffee, and walked leisurely up the final block to Starbucks. It was six-fifty when we reached the sidewalk in front of Starbucks and heard the first siren begin to wail.

"Holy shit," I said. "They've called the cops!"

"Relax," said Fox. "No way they've tumbled to

243

it yet. Bet you anything you want that that's an ambulance on the way to pick up a customer who's been inexplicably stricken with some unknown illness."

"I like that 'inexplicably stricken'!" said Clyde. "Maybe Fox should be writing the book." She smiled a wide, amoral smile that connoted no sympathy whatsoever for the possible victim or victims. I was mainly irritated by her remark about Fox writing my book, so I suppose I was equally guilty of feeling little if anything about the victims of our latest prank. It takes an amoral eye to recognize an amoral smile, I thought to myself, taking out my notebook and scribbling down the line.

"Walter is the writer," said Fox, "and I'm the fighter."

"I'm the inciter," said Clyde.

Before anyone could say another word, an obese woman in a canary yellow spandex outfit stumbled out of the front door of Starbucks and vomited on the sidewalk. Other customers continued to enter and exit the premises, generally ignoring the woman and her plight as if she were a homeless person or a dead body lying in their way.

"Good ol' New York," said Fox. "It takes more than a fat lady in neon yellow puking on a sidewalk to give anybody pause around here."

The siren was getting much louder now and as I glanced through the window, I noticed that the tempo seemed to be picking up inside the store as well. There was a guy who looked like a Wall Street type doubled up right in front of the counter, obviously suffering from rather severe bowel cramps. Other customers, however, were still placing their orders on either side of the man, as if he didn't exist.

"Not the best *latte* advertisement I can think of," said Fox, sidling up next to me by the front window. There was a smile on Fox's face resembling that of a small child opening his birthday presents.

"And look at that guy trying to get into the men's room," shrilled Clyde gleefully as she pulled up on the other side of me, encircling my waist with a slender arm.

"Here comes the first meat wagon!" said Fox as an ambulance pulled directly in front of the Starbucks. "There'll be more where that came from."

"The cops have got to get here soon," I said, trying to keep the trepidation out of my voice.

"Not necessarily," said Fox. "They haven't figured it out yet. How could they? Hell, they'll probably suspect it's some kind of weird Legionnaire's disease type of thing before they finally stumble on the truth. The truth, remember, is not only hard to take, it's often hard to find. And when they do find it, it won't make any sense to them. 'Why would anybody want to do something like this to Starbucks?' they'll say."

"Poor little Starbucks," offered Clyde.

"That's one thing they're not," said Fox. "They've got some of the deepest pockets on the whole planet. They've sucked the lifeblood out of every coffee farmer, every mom-and-pop place, and every yuppie-clone consumer in the country—"

"And they murdered the only Unicorn in New York!" finished Clyde. "They killed poor Jonjo's life's dream. They deserve whatever's coming to them!"

"And what's coming," I said, "is another ambulance."

A succession of ambulances continued to come and go for the next hour or two, and when the cops finally did show up, it appeared to be mostly in the capacity of crowd control. The largest crowd, of course, was in the immediate vicinity of the Starbucks's rest room. It was a restless and desperate and vocal crowd and it swelled and roiled and surged in front of the restroom door like the dark and dangerous tides of a distant sea—Moby-Dick's sea, if I may. People were pounding the door, kicking the door, clawing at the door, as if it were some intransigent heavenly portal representing their last and only chance for salvation. In a narrow, secular sense, no doubt, I suppose it was.

A feisty old lady was using her umbrella to push away people who were shitting and vomiting all around her. As she exited the place, she turned in our general direction and preached to the assembled multitudes: "I'm *nevah* going in there again!" she shouted. "There's something wrong with this *kaw-fee!*"

The very pavement in front of the store by this time had been transformed into an obstacle course of vomit and human excrement. People were slipping and sliding their way out of the treacherous area, some of them falling down, many others in a determined, hurried state that seemed unusual even for inveterate New Yorkers. It was a scene right out of Dante's *Inferno* all right, but I had to admit there was something genuinely funny about it, too.

"It's a Berlitz cultural-empathy course," said Fox. "There's nowhere to take a dignified crap anywhere on this block. Now they'll discover firsthand a little bit of what it's like to be homeless."

People were now flying like arrows out of Starbucks. Rubber-neckers had slowed traffic to a standstill in the area and the cops, who'd finally arrived, had their hands full with the hopelessly snarled traffic as well as moving the crowd of onlookers and kibitzers off the slippery sidewalk in front of the store. We moved on with the crowd, eventually making our way back toward the apartment. As you can imagine, we were all three in a state of high exhilaration. There was no reason then, and, indeed, I see no reason now, to pass any moral judgment upon our behavior. We did what we did for reasons I'm not sure I could explain. Maybe there was no reason. Sometimes in life that's the best reason of all.

Back at the apartment, we passed around a bottle of Jim Beam Clyde had brought, and Fox triumphantly put a little red flag on the flowchart on the wall. Then he broke out the one-hitter and started circulating that around with the Jim Beam. We were beginning to feel pretty good about things. Starbucks, for sure, had taken a major hit that morning and Clyde and Fox had lived to tell about it and I'd lived to write about it. It was not a knockout blow, however, and none of us was under the delusion that an outfit as big and deep and insidious as the Starbucks organization, or even one tiny link in its chain, could ever truly be broken. The one-eyed giant of the West could be bloodied and bowed, according to Fox, but he could never be killed. That was because, again according to Fox, he was part of every one of us.

"Today," said Fox, lying on his back in the middle of the floor, "we bore witness to a thing of beauty."

"*And* it was *fun!*" said Clyde almost wistfully. "What did you think of it all, Sunshine?"

I put my thumbs together in front of my face. Then I raised my two index fingers higher and higher toward the sky we could not see.

"Touchdown," I said.

CHAPTER 27

The next days were a little crazy and a little busy even for this intrepid trio of coconspirators. Clyde, who did not love cockroaches, nonetheless kicked into high gear in a supportive role in the operation. She began making calls to the city's health inspector's office, the same office that the Starbucks people had used to bring down the Unicorn. She complained that she'd seen cockroaches at Starbucks. There weren't, of course, any cockroaches at Starbucks. Not yet.

Clyde also, not wishing to let her antipathy for cockroaches distance her from the campaign, came up with her own plan, which eventually she named Operation Disconnect. It involved calling the *Daily News* on her untraceable phone line and placing ads for help wanted at Starbucks. The ads went out to all union and nonunion workers offering a ridiculously high hourly salary and requiring no past work experience whatsoever. Anyone interested in "exploring the possibilities of a Starbucks career" could call the number provided, which was, of course, Starbucks's number. Operation Disconnect also involved Clyde's going down to her friendly neighborhood Kinko's and making thousands of flyers, which she proceeded to put up on bulletin boards and telephone poles all over the Village. The flyers offered a one-hundred-dollar discount at Starbucks if the customer would only fax the flyer back to Starbucks with his or her address and signature included. Operation Disconnect, as you might expect, was a huge success. In some ways, I must say, Operation Disconnect, in its own quiet, unobtrusive way, was even more effective than Operation Diarrhea, if such a thing were possible. Clyde, in her own ingenious fashion, managed to bill both the newspaper ads and the flyers to Starbucks. Fox, of course, dutifully recorded Operation Disconnect on the flowchart with a little red flag.

On the morning of the second day after Operation Diarrhea, Fox walked into the apartment carrying a cardboard box of the size and shape and variety that might well contain a computer or a printer. It did not. What it contained, according to Fox, were thousands of live cockroaches he'd just purchased at the local pet shop. It also contained a net bag that secured a large and hungry gecko lizard. The bag and lizard were secured by two strings emerging from the top of the box, which, when one was pulled, would release the lizard into the population of cockroaches. Fox described all this in great detail to his audience of myself and Clyde, who appeared to be turning a whiter shade of pale.

"This weapon," said Fox, "falls into the category of organic binary munitions. Binary munitions, as you may well know, are entities that are perfectly harmless in their self-contained states. When, however, the two entities are combined, an explosion or reaction of great force takes place. Are we clear on this?"

I was fairly clear and Clyde looked so clear she was about ready to pass out. Fox bummed a quick smoke from me and continued on blithely with his narrative.

"To be fair to the cockroaches," he said, "the duct tape across the bottom few inches of the box conceals three small holes through which an avenue of escape for them is available once the tape is removed. The string is pulled first, of course, releasing the gecko; then, when the tape is removed, our little insect friends should rather quickly begin pouring out of the three holes in prodigious numbers. Clyde, for obvious reasons, will not be involved directly in Operation Cockroach Bomb, but I'd like to ask you, Walter, to participate in the same diversionary capacity in which you performed so famously before, distracting the counter people from what's going on in the center ring."

"One for all and all for one," I said. "When do we start?"

"In about five minutes," said Fox.

As Fox, his box, and I trudged down the street toward Starbucks, I began to get my first mild feelings of foreboding about the wisdom of Operation Cockroach Bomb. Maybe it was just what anybody would feel going back to the scene of his crime after only a couple of days had passed. It wasn't even really a crime, I reflected. In a world full of jury- and witness-tampering, tampering with a few sugar and syrup containers in a gourmet coffee store was pretty low on the Richter scale. Nonetheless, I must have looked a bit nervous in the service because Fox hastened to reassure me as the two of us walked the final block.

"Just be cool about it, Walter," he said. "Just do what you did last time, talk to the counter people—"

"Baristas," I corrected.

"Baristas. And I'll take care of the rest. As soon as you see me getting up to leave, you get out of there, too. Staggering our departures ever so slightly, of course."

"Of course."

"Now there is one thing you should be aware of, Walter. Starbucks by this time has for sure connected the sabotage to the dumper with the tampering with their sugars and creamers and syrups and shit. By now, they'll probably have security guards and very possibly security cameras all over the place. All this may make our job difficult but not impossible. This may, however, be the last time we can safely do any work inside the store. Operation Elephant Dump Numbers One, Two and Three, you understand, do not require our entering the store."

"Thank God for Elephant Dumps One, Two, and Three," I said.

"If God is going to be involved, Operation Cockroach Bomb is where we could really use her help. This is high-stakes poker, Walter."

Whatever Fox thought it was, it was sounding more and more like a death wish to me. The people who ran Starbucks were not idiots. They didn't know who the culprits were and they didn't know why anyone would visit this kind of sophomoric mischief upon their establishment. But surely they had been alerted by now. Surely they would never let this sort of thing happen again.

"The stakes are *too* high," I said. "Maybe we should consider folding our hand."

"History demands," said Fox, as we came upon the coffee giant, "that we ride into the Valley of the Shadow of Death sporting a large erection and a box filled with cockroaches."

With those immortal words, Fox marched into Starbucks carrying the cardboard box, with me left trailing in his wake, following along like the Village idiot. I don't contend that there was any high-minded existential credo motivating Fox or Clyde. They made no demands of Starbucks. They did not care whether or not Starbucks used nonorganic creamer. Like their true motives for doing almost everything else, I think they went to war with Starbucks just for fun, just for the hell of it, just because somebody somewhere, perhaps a very long time ago, had told them they couldn't do it.

Possibly because Fox had his hair pulled back in a ponytail and wore wire-rimmed John Denver glasses like some kind of technogeek, the new security guard at the door hardly gave him a second glance. Maybe the guard thought that a big computer box was too obvious for someone to be carrying who had his mind bent on creating havoc. There did not appear to be any security cameras installed yet, so Fox put in his order and put his box over in a far corner under an empty table. Moments later, after paying for his order, he returned to the table, sipping a *latte* and reading a magazine. I walked up to the counter, which was now manned by two men and two women, none of whom I'd seen before.

"I'll have a double espresso," I said.

"That's a *doppio*," said one of the women to the world in general.

"Right," I said. "I noticed this table over here is designed like a chessboard. Does anybody ever play chess here?"

The four baristas or whoever the hell they were did not beat each other to death answering my question. They continued to grind and pour and mix and serve their customers, one of whom was me. The woman who'd said *"doppio"* looked at me a bit quizzically, then took charity into her own hands and answered, "Not yet." This sounded like it might be my opening.

"I used to be quite a prodigy myself," I said,

engaging as many of the personnel as possible or at least partially engaging them. "When I was seven years old, I played the world grand master Samuel Reschevsky in Houston, Texas."

"No kidding," said the guy on the far right with the closest view of Fox. He didn't sound very excited about my childhood accomplishments but at least it was a human response.

"No kidding," I said, moving closer to the guy and partially blocking his field of vision. "Reschevsky played fifty people simultaneously around a huge table and he beat all of them. I happened to be the youngest of the bunch by far, and as a result I got my picture on the front page of the *Houston Chronicle*."

"Whoopee!" said the guy as he handed me my *doppio*.

"It was quite a thrill for a seven-year-old, I can tell you. Of course, it's been mostly downhill from there. One interesting thing, however, was what Samuel Reschevsky said to my father after the match. He told my dad he was sorry to have to beat his son, but he had to be very careful when he played seven-year-olds. If, by chance, he were to lose, it would be headlines. His career would be over."

"Then maybe he could come here and play at Starbucks," said the woman who'd earlier taken my order. She had such a positive tone that I could only hope she was being facetious. At least, I thought, she'd been listening.

"That might be a little difficult for him," I said. "He's been dead for thirty-five years."

"Stranger things have happened," said the other female barista. "Right here at Starbucks."

I didn't like the way she was looking at me. It was making me nervous. It was as if she knew me from somewhere but couldn't be sure. I did not dare glance in Fox's direction. Technically, I told myself, I had done nothing wrong. Whatever craziness Fox or Clyde had been up to, all I had done was tell boring stories to busy people. There was, I dimly remembered, a name for that. It was called, in legal parlance, accomplice to the crime. The woman was still looking at me as if she knew what I was thinking.

The next thing I knew I saw a ponytail heading out the front door and I knew Fox had completed the necessary steps and was getting the hell out of there. I paused for a moment or two and then turned and started to walk out of there myself. It was at just about that time that the security guard grabbed me by the shoulder. I froze physically, but my mind was running a hundred miles an hour. That's the way it happens, I thought. The main perpetrator gets away and they always catch the accomplice. Then they try to squeeze him for the identities of his cohorts. Would I rat on Fox and Clyde? It was an open question. Was I, at this very moment, sorry I'd ever met them? That was an open question, too. The only thing that didn't appear open to me was the way to get out of there.

256

This was it, I thought bitterly. Fox was long gone and the security guard was now turning me around and firmly directing me back into the store. He let go of me then and at last he spoke.

"Hey, buddy," he said. "You forgot to pick up your *doppio.*"

By the time I got back to the apartment, Fox and Clyde were already in high spirits, some of which were contained in three bottles of champagne that Clyde had procured. The celebratory mood was infectious and soon I'd forgotten all about what I'd perceived to be my close shave with Starbucks security. Fox, I noticed, had already positioned a tiny red flag on the flowchart for Operation Cockroach Bomb. Now he proceeded to provide us with a blow-by-blow account of the final stages of the operation. Clyde was squirming in her seat and looking pale again and swigging large amounts of champagne directly from the bottle, but Fox pranced along obliviously.

"When I got the box situated under a table in a corner, I pulled one of the strings, effectively removing the net bag from the box. This action, of course, released the gecko among the thousands of cockroaches and suddenly the whole box began to vibrate like—"

"A vibrator?" suggested Clyde.

"Yes. Vibrated like a vibrator. An organic binary reaction was definitely taking place. I reached down as surreptitiously as possible and pulled the duct tape off the bottom of the box, exposing the three small holes that provided escape routes for the dear little cockroaches. I wished I could have stayed longer to watch the show but, of course, I couldn't. All I can tell you is that they poured out of those holes almost with the incredible force of being shot out of a fire hose. It was a proud moment in my somewhat checkered life and it was a thing of beauty to watch. Unfortunately, I'm a very busy man and I had to get on to my next project."

"Which is?" I asked.

"Operation Elephant Dump, Numbers One, Two, and Three."

"Good!" said Clyde enthusiastically. "Finally something I can get in to."

CHAPTER 28

E lephants live a long time and they have long trunks and even longer memories. But even an elephant can't know the future. All he can do is try not to be haunted by his memories. Thus it was that Operation Elephant Dump Numbers One, Two, and Three took a little more time and planning than the array of other puerile pranks performed against our mutual enemy that was Starbucks. The three phases of the Elephant Dump operation would prove to be some of the most ingenious and effective of the entire campaign, but they would also require Fox's being out of the apartment a great deal, rounding up the appropriate supplies and equipment. This was not, entirely in itself, a bad thing. It gave Clyde and myself a chance to explore the possibilities of a career in petty crime together, as well as lending the pretty fair illusion at times that the two of us were keeping house together. That illusion was shattered periodically, however, by Fox's coming in during the early hours of the dawn, usually drunk or stoned or both, and nattering on about his progress regarding Operation Elephant Dump, Numbers One, Two, and Three.

But there were lots of times when, for lengthy and very pleasant periods, Clyde and I were alone together. Maybe "alone together" is not the best way to phrase it, for it was better than that. True, we had yet to be sexually intimate with each other. But with Clyde, and occasionally, the peripatetic Fox, living in a virtual slumber party at my apartment, it seemed to me that the three of us had never been closer. Because it was war, and also for sheer convenience, we had decided to quite literally go to the mattresses. Clyde and I each slept on our own mattress side by side on the floor and Fox slept on the other side of Clyde in his sleeping bag. When Fox was out wandering the night, Clyde and I managed to pursue a good bit of drinking, laughing, cuddling, and some of the nicest pillow talk in my life. The fact that we had not yet technically made love bothered me a bit, but it was more than compensated for by how close Clyde and I were growing to each other. We shared our dreams, our toothpaste, our drinks, and sometimes even our mattresses. Given time, I knew we would make it.

So that's what we were doing. Living together in a very exciting, romantic, bohemian, revolutionary, ridiculous style. Clyde was smoking, having fun, looking beautiful with that twinkling haze of mischief forever in her eyes. I was typing, editing, making notes to myself, all those things that authors routinely do, and it didn't seem to be bothering Clyde anymore. Maybe she had finally resigned herself to the fact that I was going to write the book and that there was nothing anybody, including myself, could do about it. Fox was my lone voice of encouragement. When he wasn't busy filling up the flowchart with little red flags, he would often ask me what page I was on. I would say, for instance, page 187, and he would say "Good. Good. Keep at it." I don't think he ever once looked at any of the words I was writing. Maybe he thought that words were not really all that important. I believe he thought that a man of words is a straw man, a man who spends words like dollars and doesn't really have anything to show for it, not even peace of mind. Maybe he thought that words were pathetic little creatures, cockroaches without legs, particles of sand swirling on an empty beach, until taken together they come to represent vital, shining, immortal things like moments, dreams, and madness.

And how was Starbucks coping with this peculiar onslaught of craziness? Well, Starbucks was Starbucks and nothing seemed to faze it or give it pause or slow its cheerful, inexorable, cancerlike growth. Clyde and I, at her instigation, of course, even went in and had a nice cup of cappuccino together one morning. Clyde always liked to live dangerously and I learned that I liked to be around people who liked to live dangerously. It was, in fact, a pretty good cup of cappuccino. There were no signs of cockroaches, Clyde was relieved to find. There were no video cameras in position. There were still no chess pieces on the board. No players, either, but lots of customers. Phone lines and faxes, I was sure, had already been rerouted and several security guards could be seen loitering about the place, looking fairly bored. It's hard to stop a thing like Starbucks and I don't even know why anybody in their right mind would want to try. It could have been my imagination, or possibly I'm attributing human qualities to dull, corporate entities, but the Starbucks store itself seemed almost stoic in the face of our pesky campaign of persistent harassment. I didn't mention it to Clyde. She would have thought I was crazy. She would have said I was feeling sorry for Starbucks. I might, indeed, have been crazy, but I certainly wasn't feeling sorry for Starbucks. I have too great a capacity for feeling sorry for myself to ever feel sorry for anyone else. Every author who fancies himself worthy of the gutter indulges in this self-pitying tissue of horseshit from time to time.

Because of the time constraints, and because I don't want to kill too many trees in America, I have arbitrarily decided to condense Operation Elephant Dump, Numbers One, Two, and Three into one rather abbreviated chapter. My editor, Steve Samet, later complained bitterly about this, insisting that each elephant dump was unique and essential and should therefore be properly framed in its own individual chapter. I wouldn't hear of it, of course. The novel had to be reined in somewhere, I maintained. Otherwise, it might become as wild, orgiastic, and out of control as some of the characters who lived and breathed, loved foolishly, and did many famous and impractical things between the sheets we've come to call pages. ("Personally, I'd never read this shit," I told Samet. "It's bad enough I have to write it." "At least," he said, "you don't have to edit it." "Don't get me wrong," I continued. "The only reason I denigrate my own work is because it shadows life too faithfully. If *The Great Armenian Novel* sucks, it's simply because life does." "I agree," said Samet. "Why do you think I live with three cats and wear a bow tie?")

Anyway, enough about little people and their silly jobs. An army of authors, editors, agents, publishers, copy editors, lawyers, publicists, and critics would never have the madness and courage required to wage battle with the one-eyed giant. Well, maybe certain authors would have tried such a stunt but they're all dead, most of them choosing to die in gutters, arranging for pauper's graves in which to be buried, hoping for the immortality that eludes us all in life. But Fox and Clyde were characters in every sense of the word, characters with character. They leaped off the page with a reckless life force right up the asshole of America.

Fox walked into the apartment late one night while Clyde was holding both my hands and searching my eyes for something I don't think she ever found. Fox's pockets were making little clinking sounds like many tiny Lilliputians toasting a damned fine effort by Jonathan Swift. Fox extracted a number of small bottles, each filled with a clear liquid. He proceeded to commandeer from under the kitchen sink a spray bottle that I'd forgotten I had, empty the contents, and pour each of the little bottles into the larger receptacle.

"What is it?" I asked.

"Elephant Dump Number One," he said. "Butyric acid."

"It certainly smells like an elephant dump," observed Clyde.

"You have no idea what this stuff will smell like once I spray it on the front wall of Starbucks," said Fox. "People will be avoiding the entire West Village. Intrepid or misguided tourists will be dropping like flies. Flies ought to like it, though."

"When does this operation get under way?" I inquired.

"In about five minutes," said Fox.

"Good," said Clyde. "That's some nasty shit and I'd like to get it out of here."

"I don't really need any help on Dump Number One," said Fox. "But you two can come along as UN observers if you like."

"Might get some good material," said Clyde facetiously, looking at me still.

"Wouldn't miss it for the world," I said.

By the time we got to Starbucks, it was almost three o'clock in the morning, a good hour if you were spraying butyric acid on the front of a Starbucks. Clyde and I served as lookouts for

Fox and the whole operation took slightly less than three minutes. There was, I must report, not much to see. There was, however, a startlingly appalling amount to smell. As we walked away from the scene, the malodorous aroma seemed to almost pursue our rapid footsteps down the street. We could still smell the horrible stench a block away.

"That ought to give a few soccer moms a second thought about going in for their morning *latte*," said Fox, with a wickedly happy smile.

"Jesus," said Clyde. "That'll give the hunchback of Notre Dame a second thought."

"They'll have to close down tomorrow," I said.

"You'd be surprised," said Fox. "They're pretty enterprising. Maybe the baristas will give each customer a gas mask so they can avoid going without their indispensable, wonderful, fucking favorite gourmet blend."

"Do I detect a bit of bitterness in your tone?" asked Clyde sweetly.

"Not bitterness," said Fox. "Only sadness and rage. There are elements of sadness and rage behind everything that's ever been funny in this world."

"Then the joke's on all of us," I said.

"Good. Good," said Fox. "Keep writing."

I don't know if Starbucks opened or not that morning. I had to hand it to them, however. They took a licking and kept right on ticking. As for us, the three partners in crime, we slept in until well past noon. I lay there on my mattress on the floor watching Clyde sleep like an angel next to me and listening to Fox snoring in his sleeping bag on the other side of her. The devil in his sleeping bag. Sometimes your mind can be so clear when you first wake up that if you just lie there half thinking, half dreaming, you begin to think you're a different person. It's almost like seeing yourself and your life and your friends for the first time. The shenanigans we were foisting on Starbucks, I thought, were juvenile, inane, and futile to the extreme and yet the whole ludicrous campaign seemed to shimmer in my mind with excitement and danger and fun. No one could ever have talked you into something this crazy. You had to want to be a part of it. Ours is not to reason why, I thought. Ours is just to do or die. Was Clyde an angel and Fox a devil, or had they both simply become internalized living parts of myself?

Why were we doing what we were doing? That was a question the cops would have to ask if they ever caught us. I'm still not sure there was really an answer, but I'll try to give you one. Fox was doing it mostly on principle. Clyde was doing it mostly for fun. And my motives, I'm afraid, were not quite as pure. I was not doing it for the hell of it, a notion that drove practically everything Fox and Clyde ever did in their lives. I was scheming against Starbucks for cynical, vicarious, practical reasons, and almost all of them by this time revolved around what Clyde had once called "that bloody book." She had not been wrong. More blood would soon be poured onto its pages than any of us could have suspected.

I did not see Elephant Dump Number Two. I stayed home writing that night, but Fox and Clyde told me all about it when they got back just before dawn. It had been, apparently, at least according to Fox, "a thing of real beauty." Clyde had come in the door looking as if she'd just had an orgasm. Maybe she had.

"Oh, Sunshine!" she gushed. "You really should have been there!"

"We could've used you for a lookout," said Fox. "The cops were all over the neighborhood, like flies."

"So were the flies," said Clyde.

"We had to wait until almost four-thirty to bring in the truck," said Fox.

"What truck?" I asked.

"Septic-tank truck I sort of borrowed," said Fox. "Holds five thousand gallons of raw sewage."

"I got to ride shotgun!" said Clyde.

Starbucks, indubitably, now realized that these pranks were far from random acts of vandalism. They well knew that a concerted campaign of no-holds-barred, rather sophomoric insanity was being diabolically waged against them for reasons, I'm sure, they could hardly fathom. But they, assuredly, as we learned from occasional reconnaissance missions in the following days, did not plan to go down without a fight. More security guards, more cops, more sanitation people, and always more baristas were brought aboard to replace those who had succumbed to the stench. Customers had to choose on any given morning between their desire for *mocha latte* and their desire not to gag before they walked in the door. But after a few more days, the place was amazingly right back to its sanitized, antiseptic, spiritually cauterized self. Fox, who could walk out on a limb in a hurricane with the best of them, felt it was time to stand down for a few days. The attacks had been coming fairly fast and furiously and we couldn't expect to get away with it for much longer. Unmarked squad cars could now be seen cruising by the front of Starbucks in twenty-minute intervals, twenty-four hours a day. We had to change our tactics or it would be only a matter of time before the game would be up. But Fox's sense of completion got the best of him. He wanted to work in Elephant Dump Number Three before we took a hiatus.

"Of course, we can't get *real* elephant shit," he said one afternoon as the three of us shared a large pepperoni pizza in the apartment. "I've contacted the circus and it's just not practical. In order to get enough, we'd have to follow the circus from town to town with an elephant wheeler."

"It's probably highly perishable, too," said Clyde, favoring me with a broad wink.

"So I've talked to a stable in Westchester and it looks like we're going to have to settle for horseshit."

"I hate it when that happens," I said.

"We'll requisition a Ryder truck," said Fox. "We'll line it with heavy canvas. We'll go to the stables and fill it up. Should hold, if my calculations are correct, a little under a ton. Then one night later this week we'll deposit the load in a lightninglike maneuver on the sidewalk right in front of Starbucks."

"How do we do that?" I asked. "It's not a dump truck."

"Permit me to hold on to some of my trade secrets," said Fox. "You'll find out in very short order."

"I don't know about dumping a ton of horseshit on the sidewalk," said Clyde.

"*Almost* a ton," Fox corrected.

"I don't think it's a very nice thing to do to the garbagemen who'll have to clean it up," she said.

"Ah, but that's the sweet part," Fox continued. "The city sanitation department will never agree to remove a ton of horseshit on the sidewalk."

"*Almost* a ton," Clyde said sweetly.

"It's something in their bylaws," Fox went on. "They won't touch it for love or money. Starbucks will have to hire their own private carting firm, you know, the Linguini Brothers or something, and that's really going to cost them. They'll be at the mercy of the horseshit mafia, but it's the only way they're ever going to get it out of there."

"Sounds like a plan," I said encouragingly.

Actually, it sounded like sheer madness but it did represent the kind of cinematic action sequence that Sylvia Lowell had found so lacking in my manuscript. Even I, as an author, could appreciate that Hollywood would not love many chapters of conversations between three crazy people temporarily keeping their heads down in a basement apartment. I could appreciate what Hollywood wanted but I wasn't going to give them what they wanted. Besides, I reckoned, when was the last time anyone in Hollywood actually read a book? No self-respecting author should ever write for Hollywood. You shouldn't write for the Sylvia Lowells or the Steve Samets of the world either. And especially, whatever you do, you should never write for yourself. In fact, if you're going to write at all, you might as well write for the customers of Starbucks. They are the mindless, faceless, meaningless mainstream without whom no author or artist can be successful. They are the ones, between the sidewalk and the stars, between the windmill and the world, who let Mozart, Van Gogh, Oscar Wilde, Edgar Allan Poe, Anne Frank, and Jesus die in the gutters of eternity.

Time glided by quickly and softly on dragonfly wings. Fox got the truck and the horseshit. Clyde and I took in a few movies, had a romantic candlelit dinner in a small Italian restaurant, and walked hand in hand blithely and blamelessly through the little sun-dappled streets of the Village. By the appointed night, however, all of us seemed more than ready for Operation Elephant Dump Number Three. Fox, as aware as anybody that the heat would be intense, had already schemed with Teddy and a group of homeless people to stage a well-timed diversion at a point several blocks away from Starbucks. We waited on a side street in the Ryder truck and, when the sirens had all passed us by, we moved on the target. In no time, we were backed up to the sidewalk in front of Starbucks and Fox and I, wearing gloves and overalls he'd requisitioned for the project, got out of the truck and tied two strong ropes to the base of a nearby lamppost. Clyde waited in the cab of the truck with instructions to signal us if a cop came by, but none did. I don't know what we would have done if one had, but these are the chances you take in the life you live. Ninety seconds later, Clyde pulled carefully away from the curb, allowing the ropes and the heavy canvas to deposit, with a large, deep, soft whumping sound, slightly less than one ton of horseshit onto the sidewalk in front of Starbucks. Sixty seconds later, we had the rope and canvas back inside the now-horseshitless truck and we were out of there.

Fox dropped Clyde and me off at the apartment and drove off to get rid of the truck somewhere. I immediately took a shower and when I got out was mildly surprised to find Clyde, wearing only a bra and panties, sitting in the middle of the floor with the one-hitter and a bottle of expensive cognac. Three full glasses were positioned around her on the floor. She'd just taken a deep hit off the one-hitter and was patting the floor next to her, smiling through the smoke. Modest fellow that I was, I put on some jeans and proceeded to share the one-hitter and the cognac. I remember at one point she kissed me and I could taste the cognac on her lips all the way to the depths of my soul.

By the time Fox returned several hours later, all of us were walking on our knuckles. Fox, after dropping off the truck, had stopped by a small park and passed around a few bottles of cheap wine with Teddy and his friends. Somewhere during that time they had concocted the grand scheme that was to be the climax of the campaign against Starbucks. Fox refused to divulge the precise nature of the plan except to say that the principal figure of the operation was, indeed, Teddy. After some cajoling from myself and Clyde, Fox still steadfastly refused to reveal the inner workings of what he called "the greatest little adventure of them all." He preferred, he said, for both of us to observe it as it unfolded, to bear witness to a carefully crafted spontaneous action of which neither of us was involved in the planning stages.

"It always makes for more compelling reading, Walter," he said, "when the author himself is unaware of how the story ends."

So I went into it unaware of the plan, unaware of what would happen, and unaware that it would be the last time the three of us would ever be together.

CHAPTER 29

What you're reading now I pieced together after the fact, partly from what I witnessed myself and partly from little comments made in passing by Fox or Clyde. I don't know how Fox got Starbucks to hire Teddy, but they did. If they'd gone into his record for about twenty seconds, I feel certain they wouldn't have touched him with a barge pole. Maybe a new resumé was created just for Teddy so they'd hire him. Anyway, they did, because we could see his large, dark form moving back and forth occasionally near the front windows. Sometimes Teddy would wave to me and motion for me to come into the place, but after Elephant Dump Numbers Two and Three, I felt it was the better part of valor not to darken Starbucks's door.

This went on for about a week and things seemed pretty quiet. The horseshit, of course, had all been cleaned up and carted away at Starbucks's expense by the Linguini Brothers or whoever the hell it is who carts large piles of horseshit away from gourmet coffee shops. Clyde probably knew more about what Fox was up to than I did. Maybe he'd confided in her and told her the whole plan. I don't know and I'll most likely never know and I suppose that in any way it really doesn't much matter. Fox was right about rage and sadness being just beneath the surface of things people often think of as funny. He was wrong, however, in not foreseeing what sometimes happens when you play with people's lives. I'm not getting up on a moral soapbox here because I'm as guilty as Fox, maybe more so, depending on how you look at it. These days, of course, I prefer not to. Like Starbucks customers, there'll always be plenty of guilt to go around.

As near as I can figure it, here's how the whole fiasco went down. Through some nefarious connection or quirk of fate, Mordecai Hoffman, an Orthodox Jewish firebrand and rabble-rouser, received information that the new Starbucks location was situated precisely upon the site of one of the first Jewish cemeteries in New York. Whether or not this bit of historical trivia was correct is probably not relevant now and it certainly wasn't relevant to Mordecai Hoffman. Mordecai, like many self-styled political and/or religious leaders of the day, was forever looking for a cause to get behind, and a parade to get in front of. He jumped like a Cossack onto the Jewish cemetery issue, and soon there were all manner of half-baked, biblical-looking Orthodox rabbis along with a ragged, but rabid, group of zealous followers showing up daily to picket Starbucks. This, of course, though quite a colorful sight to see, did little to deter the stubborn

Starbucks aficionados from reveling in life, liberty, and the pursuit of a decaf *mocha latte*.

When I think about it, I know it had to be Fox who slipped the little cemetery tidbit to Hoffman because what happened next was about as clear an example of an organic binary munition as was humanly possible to create. This was because its components were not comprised of cockroaches and gecko lizards. The organic binary munition was comprised of two highly divergent groups of human beings. The first element was the afore-mentioned band of Orthodox Jewish picketers and troublemakers. The second element—well, I'll get to the second element in just a moment.

First, though, there had to be a triggering mecha-nism, which was Teddy getting fired. This, quite naturally, was no surprise to anybody except, of course, Teddy.

It happened one afternoon about a week after Elephant Dump Number Three, and I suppose it happened for the same inviolate reasons everything else happens in this world: "Between the gutter and the stars, people are what people are." You can't blame Teddy for being Teddy and you can't blame the people at Starbucks for being the people at Starbucks. It is the way of their people; it is the way of all people. Anyway, there was, presumably, some sort of misunderstanding, which led in turn to some kind of altercation. Maybe Teddy suddenly started believing he was mixing a secret, sacred, traditional kava potion for a manhood ritual among South Pacific Islanders. Maybe he thought that as king of his imaginary African kingdom, he was entitled to compensation for sales of all Kenyan and Tanzanian gourmet coffee blends. Maybe his wig just snapped from the tedium and the ennui of working every day at Starbucks. For whatever reason, two burly security guards, who looked like midgets on either side of Teddy, escorted him out of the place that afternoon right through the throng of cheering Orthodox Jewish protesters who'd mistaken him for a black Jew from Ethiopia who they assumed had been involved in an act of passive resistance. Everyone thought that was the end of it, of course. Everyone but Fox.

The following evening around nine o'clock, at Fox's instigation, I drifted by Starbucks to witness what Fox had said would be "The Show." Clyde, I noticed, was already there, smoking a cigarette, drinking a non-Starbucks coffee, and carrying on an animated discussion with Mordecai Hoffman. I did not see Fox anywhere, but shortly after nine, Teddy showed up surrounded by the other element in the organic binary munition: about two dozen Black Muslims, all decked out in black suits, white shirts, black bow ties, and funny-looking black monkey hats that ironically did not appear to be vastly dissimilar to the ones some of the Orthodox Jews were sporting.

"Jesus," said Clyde, who'd found her way over to me. "*This* ought to be good."

"Did you know this was going to happen?" I asked.

"I didn't know any more about it than you did," she said. "It just sprang out of the whole cloth of Fox's mind, I guess. He wanted me to see whatever is going to happen with 'fresh eyes,' he said. Maybe he thinks I'm going to write a book."

"Are you?"

"One author in the family is quite enough, Walter. Isn't this *fun?*"

"Well, it *is*—um—interesting, certainly at least in a sociological sense."

"Brighten up, Sunshine," she said, putting her hand on my cheek. "Give me a kiss."

"Give you a kiss?" I said incredulously. "There's about to be a race riot with the possibility of blood in the streets, and you want a kiss?"

"What better time for a kiss?" she asked, with an innocence that actually caused a pang in my heart.

The night was already dark and the mood was turning dark and I kissed her long, deeply, and lovingly, and wondered again about this odd, charming, streetwise girl I was kissing. When I finally came up for air, I noticed that the leader of the Black Muslims, whom I subsequently learned was named Jabreel X, was leading his troops through the crowd of Jews into the Land of Milk and Honey, which, in this case, was Starbucks. I would not exactly say the Jews parted like the Red Sea, but it must be reported that the Black Muslims enjoyed a relatively unimpeded progression through the crowd and into the store. Once inside, they stood around and glowered at patrons in surly fashion while Jabreel X sought out the store manager to inquire about the circumstances of Teddy's termination from his recent employment. It is not a pleasant thing for your average yuppie customer to suddenly turn around and see two dozen Black Muslims standing casually around, not ordering anything but paranoia and bad vibrations. All politics and social commentary aside, it's just not good for business.

Clyde and I moved in a little closer and we could see the store manager and Jabreel X huddled together in what appeared to be a serious, rational posture. Jabreel X did not need to make threats, of course. With a store full of Black Muslims loitering about, Jabreel X could be saying he wanted a tin of breath mints and still seem threatening. Clyde and I watched. The Jewish picketers watched. A small but growing crowd of spectators watched. Even a few cops pulled up in a squad car and watched. The discussion appeared to be going on interminably and so the cops did not move in. No laws, evidently, were being broken and no one had called for help. Then, a rather bizarre incident occurred. Teddy, obviously growing bored with the conversation between Jabreel X and the store manager, proceeded to tie what appeared to be a bright green Starbucks apron or tablecloth around his neck like a cape or a royal cloak. Then, grabbing an empty sixteen-ounce coffee cup and placing it upside down upon his head, he began marching regally around the store, exhorting and issuing apparent commands we could not hear to the few remaining customers and to the Black Muslims, who appeared to be dumbfounded by this unexpected, aberrant, and totally undignified behavior.

"Oh, Teddy," said Clyde.

It didn't take long for Jabreel X and his followers to realize that they'd been had, and that the mild-mannered black man they'd championed, who'd lost his job at Starbucks and was now marching around like a king in a storybook, was obviously cooking on another planet. The Black Muslims, looking to the man as chagrined and sheepish as it is possible for a Black Muslim to look, filed quickly out of the store, but this time the Red Sea didn't seem to part quite so easily.

It started with a bit of pushing and shoving, continued with some name-calling, and before anybody knew it, the sidewalk in front of Starbucks was the scene of a full-blown melee.

More cops had appeared on the scene, but the action was clearly beginning to spill over into the street, with Mordecai Hoffman and Jabreel X commanding like field generals their opposing armies of the night. And the cops were caught in the middle of the fray. Fists were flying, people were being shoved to the ground, and the front window of Starbucks was shattered by a skinny Lubavitch Jew swinging a picket sign over his head like a human helicopter. In the midst of this churning cauldron of depravity, there gradually materialized two figures I recognized: Fox Harris, who was standing on the fringe of the mob, arguing with a cop, and Teddy, who was just now descending majestically from the doorway of Starbucks as if he expected a royal coach to be waiting for him. I had half dragged Clyde across the street and, against her wishes, we were watching the scene from the relatively safe vantage point of the opposite sidewalk.

"Oh, Teddy," she whispered. "Stay inside."

"There's Fox arguing with the cops."

"I'm going back over there," said Clyde defiantly.

"You're staying right here," I said, encircling her in my arms.

"Let me go, Walter!" she screamed.

But now there was no place to go. Cops were suddenly pouring out of the woodwork, separating the warring factions, and arresting the unruly masses, most of whom just as suddenly began fleeing into the night. Indeed, a small cordon of cops had rapidly formed directly in front of us, effectively sealing off any attempt at approach by Clyde or myself. So we watched with fresh eyes as the cops placed Fox in handcuffs and hustled him out of there in the back of a squad car. We watched as Teddy walked obliviously toward the cops, ignoring their commands to stop. We watched as they hammered him with nightsticks and sprayed him with pepper spray.

And yet he seemed to shake it off, standing for a moment alone, like a wounded bear in the light of a streetlamp. Then he turned and charged the cops. Gunfire crackled in the cold night. Then Teddy fell to the sidewalk.

Clyde turned away, burying her head in my chest, sobbing convulsively, then breaking into a long and lonely wail that found its only counterpoint in the sirens of an approaching ambulance. After a short period of time, they put a sheet on Teddy and pulled it over his head. After a little more time, they carried him off, put him in the meat wagon, and took him away.

Soon the night became very quiet, indeed. Almost all you could hear was the sound of traffic on the avenues, like the muted drumming of the warriors from some imaginary African kingdom.

CHAPTER 30

The best people you'll ever meet will often come to you like stray dogs and cats, moving with graceful evanescence through your life, then leaving you forever with empty spaces that only you can fill. After Teddy's death, I saw Fox and Clyde only one more time, then they moved on to the streets and alleyways of the world, leaving me no choice but to relegate them to the blameless pages of the manuscript in progress, nearing completion, but in a larger sense, never really ending. About four nights after the disaster at Starbucks, Fox came by my apartment. As you can imagine, I was quite surprised to see him. He hugged me as he came in the door. He looked pale and wan and a bit shaky but he still had that infectious, world-beating smile. This time, however, the smile did not seem quite able to reach up into his eyes.

"How's the book coming?" he asked, immediately breaking out the one-hitter and the locket filled with Malabimbi Madness.

"Fox!" I shouted. "How'd you get out of jail?"

"Clyde brought me a copy of your manuscript with a hacksaw in it."

"Then you know I'm almost finished."

"I am, too," said Fox.

I smoked more dope with Fox that night than I ever have in my life, before or since, and when we were through, he gave me the one-hitter and the silver locket, like a man on his deathbed passing on the most precious trinkets of his existence. It was almost two in the morning when he got up to leave. He stopped at the door and asked me if I wanted to go for a little ride.

"Where'd you get the car?" I asked as I followed him outside.

"Same place I got the Ryder truck," he said.

I guess you'd expect an author to have an eye for detail, but I couldn't tell you what kind of car it was that Fox had evidently "requisitioned." It was a late model, it was a dark car, and it was a dark night. That's about all I remember except that I got in and Fox started cruising slowly around the neighborhood. I was out of cigarettes and I mentioned that fact to Fox.

"Check the glove compartment," he said.

I opened the glove compartment and found a pack of cigarettes. I also found a gun.

"Jesus, Fox," I said. "Where'd you get this gun?"

"Came with the car," he said.

Fox drove around for a while longer, then stopped along the curb across the street from where Teddy had died in front of Starbucks. The window had been fixed, I noticed. Starbucks looked dark and deserted. The whole street looked dark and deserted. Suddenly, I was overwhelmed with a cold and unforgiving rage that came from somewhere deeper in my dark and deserted soul than I ever cared to know about. I opened the glove compartment, took out the gun, and lowered my passenger-side window. The night air came into the car and it was cold and unforgiving, too. It was a one-way street and it was a one-way life and you do it their way or you don't do it at all. There was nothing between me and Starbucks now. There never had been anything between me and Starbucks. I aimed the gun at the Starbucks window and I fired methodically six times, shattering the glass again. Then Fox took the gun away from me, rubbing off my fingerprints with his own hands, placing it back in the glove compartment. He quickly pulled away from the curb and drove me back to my apartment. He checked in the rearview several times but there was no sign of cops. As I got out of the car, in front of my building, Fox leaned over from the wheel and uttered the last words I would ever hear him say.

"You know something, Walter," he said. "You're all right."

It was late the following afternoon when I finally got up, wandered over to a nearby little Greek coffee shop, and read the newspaper. "Two Killed in Drive-by Shooting at Starbucks," it said. Employees working late, repairing damage from previous protests. Suspect apprehended with murder weapon bearing his fingerprints. Suspect makes full confession to the police.

CHAPTER 31

That night Clyde came over with her suitcase. She said she was shipping out. Things were getting too hot since Fox's arrest. There was a moment when I saw the sparkle in her eyes, dimmed recently by tears, during which I almost told her who the real triggerman was. But that moment passed and I let it. It was then that I truly felt Clyde and Fox slipping through the fingers of my life, consigned, for better or worse, to the pages of a book. What was it that Fox once said? I asked myself. "The only things you really keep in life are the things you let slip through your fingers." Something like that.

"There's not much time," she said, taking off her clothes. "I've got a plane to catch in a few hours."

"You're not traveling like that, I hope."

"That's very funny, Walter. Your wit seems to have sharpened noticeably in the time you've been around Fox and myself."

"How could it not?" I said truthfully.

"Aren't you going to take your clothes off?"

"Well," I said, fumbling with a button on my shirt.

"There's not time to be modest, Sunshine. This is something you've been wanting to do for a long time now."

She turned off the lamp on my desk and the room took on an almost subterranean dimness, bathing her skin with the ambient glow of the light from the street. Bending gracefully, like a tree in a storm, she removed two religious candles from her purse, placed them carefully on the windowsill, and borrowing my lighter for one last time, she lit them reverentially, prayerfully, in the manner of a supplicant at the altar of a god she trusted in spite of everything. The candlelight touched her skin like fireflies, like roses, like little fingers of light and lightness through which would slip a memory I would surely keep.

"Take off your clothes, Walter," she ordered in a soft, husky voice, and I obeyed.

"Get on the floor," she said.

And I did. And she was on top of me, fucking my brains out, sitting on my face, sucking my cock like a Dreamsicle on a dusty summer day. And I was all over her, wanting her love, her passion, her scent to stay with me forever. And on it went, her fingers pulling my hair, her fingernails raking my back, her very essence becoming a part of me as our bodies rolled across the floor in the flickering shadows of the candlelight. After we came together, we slept in each other's arms, with me still inside her, wanting more, wanting everything, wanting what I knew I would never have again.

When we woke from our little reverie, we dressed quickly and spoke briefly in oddly hushed tones. She talked of going to South America. I talked of completing the novel, editing, book tours. She had looked beautiful without any clothes on and she looked just as beautiful standing at the door with her suitcase in her hand. I believed I saw a bit more of that old sparkle back in her eyes. It made me happy to see it.

"I promise you I'll always be a vegetarian," I said.

"I know you will," said Clyde.

"The two religious candles," I said. "Are they for Fox and Teddy?"

"They're just for two chirpies," she said.

"Chirpies?"

"Two birds. They could be for Fox and Teddy. They could be for the two people who Fox didn't know were inside Starbucks when he shot up the place like a crazy cowboy. They could be for Fox and me, who once were your partners in crime and now are your creations."

I didn't say a word. I just stood there and watched the candlelight dancing in her eyes.

"The candles could be for you and me, Walter. They could be for all of us."

She opened the door and she walked out into the little hallway. I think there were tears in her eyes.

"Or they could just be," she said, "for any two birds who want to fly."

CHAPTER 32

A year has passed since the night Clyde left and a lot of things have happened in the parallel worlds of fiction and nonfiction. I finished the book almost before Clyde's candles burned out and, believe it or not, it immediately started leaping off bookshelves all over the country. One critic actually said: "The characters leap off the page." In the process, I've made quite a leap myself. I've moved from the old basement apartment in the Village to a large, airy, spacious place overlooking Central Park. And why not? I can certainly afford it. At this writing, not only are book and author doing well, the book's on the best-seller list and Sylvia Lowell is telling everybody that Walter Snow's a genius and she knew it the whole time. Steve Samet loves me, too, and now Hollywood's considering turning the book into a movie except they want the three central characters to be black and they want Teddy to be white and they want the story set in a small town in rural Mississippi. They do like the Starbucks angle, however. As they were quick to point out, even small towns in rural Mississippi have a Starbucks these days.

Fox is on death row, and this bothers me sometimes but there's nothing I can do about it. I haven't visited him or spoken to him since the night he was arrested but I do have my reasons. For one thing, he might decide to change his story, but I don't worry about that too much because nobody would believe him. The other reason I don't feel guilty about not visiting him is because I've already admitted in the book that I shot the people in Starbucks. No one believes it, of course, because the book is fiction and no one believes fiction even if it's the truth.

I have agreed nonetheless, through lawyers, that I would go along with Fox's request that I take formal custody of his tropical fish, which are now swimming around in a large aquarium in my large living room. They don't seem to care much whether they're in a basement apartment or a penthouse. In an odd way, neither do I. I've got the one-hitter still and the silver locket and a large supply of the best dope in town and I find myself smoking a lot these days and watching Fox's fish. Tropical fish don't really belong in New York, I think, any more than we do. They should be swimming around in some beautiful coral reef in some crystal-clear tropical ocean. Instead, they just swim round and round in their glass-enclosed prison until they drown in their own sorrows like the rest of us poor bastards. But don't get the idea I'm not happy. It's just that when you're successful, important, and famous, happy doesn't really come into the picture.

Oh yeah, I almost forgot. I got a postcard from Clyde this afternoon. First time I've heard from her. No return address. I miss Clyde. Sometimes when I get stoned, I miss her so much I almost forget to feed the fish. Sometimes I think I should have gone with Clyde instead of going to cocktail parties and late dinners at Elaine's and then out on book tours. I miss Clyde. I miss Fox, too. And I miss who I was when I was with them. But I'm not that person anymore and maybe I never was and anyway I can't afford to be. Now all I do is feed Fox's fucking fish, sign checks, and inscribe books to people who tell me I have a wonderful imagination. Can you imagine that?

Anyway, here's Clyde's postcard. Here. I'll read it to you.

Dear Walter,

I live on a secluded island called Moro de Sao Paulo off the coast of Brazil. My heart is happy here. My soul is at peace. I don't think I'm coming back. I wish you all the success in the world.

Love,

Clyde

P.S. I have a beautiful baby boy now. His name is Walter. He's almost three months old. Sometimes I call him Sunshine.

ACKNOWLEDGMENTS

The divine spirit within the author salutes the divine spirit within his agent, David Vigliano. The author would also like to express his gratitude to the editors who worked on this book: Mauro DiPreta, Joelle Yudin, and Diane Reverand. Thanks also go to Ted Mann and Goat Carson. The author extends a special salute to the memories of Fox Harris (Peace be with you, Fox) and Clyde Potts (Wherever you are).